Noah leaned forward, his words a whisper across her temple.

"You're safe with me, Princess. You have my word. Nothing will happen that you don't want to happen."

Her breath hitched at the thought of what she'd like to happen. It was unprecedented to hunger like this for any man.

Ilsa tried to tell herself she was simply feeling bruised and rejected and Noah's blatant interest was a balm to her battered ego. But the real truth swamped that totally.

The truth was she'd never in her life been drawn to anyone like this. Every cell in her body screamed that it would be criminal, impossible even, to turn away.

She moistened her lips and saw his gaze flicker and sizzle.

"It's Ilsa. Don't call me Princess."

His sculpted mouth tilted up at the corners and that hint of appreciation undid another knot in the fabric of her defensive caution.

How would his lips feel against hers? Hot and decadent or coolly delicious?

Growing up near the beach, **Annie West** spent lots of time observing tall, burnished lifeguards—early research! Now she spends her days fantasizing about gorgeous men and their love lives. Annie has been a reader all her life. She also loves travel, long walks, good company and great food. You can contact her at annie@annie-west.com or via PO Box 1041, Warners Bay, NSW 2282, Australia.

Books by Annie West

Harlequin Presents

Claiming His Out-of-Bounds Bride
The Sheikh's Marriage Proclamation
Pregnant with His Majesty's Heir
A Consequence Made in Greece
The Innocent's Protector in Paradise

Sovereigns and Scandals

Revelations of a Secret Princess
The King's Bride by Arrangement

Visit the Author Profile page
at Harlequin.com for more titles.

Annie West

—

CLAIMING HIS VIRGIN PRINCESS

Recycling programs
for this product may
not exist in your area.

ISBN-13: 978-1-335-56840-3

Claiming His Virgin Princess

This edition published by arrangement with Harlequin Books S.A.

For questions and comments about the quality of this book,
please contact us at CustomerService@Harlequin.com.

Harlequin Enterprises ULC
22 Adelaide St. West, 41st Floor
Toronto, Ontario M5H 4E3, Canada
www.Harlequin.com

Printed in U.S.A.

CLAIMING HIS VIRGIN PRINCESS

With special thanks to my friend Reeze.

For iced coffees and problem-solving on hot summer days.

For laughs over life's sillinesses.

For braving rapacious kookaburras for the greater good.

And for all the rest...

PROLOGUE

'HE MIGHT BE HANDSOME, but I hate him. How could he hurt our Princess like that? She's so nice and now he's broken her heart and she's miserable—'

'Shh! She'll be here any second,' another girl hissed. 'It's almost time and she's never late.'

Out in the corridor of the children's ward Ilsa felt her heartbeat quicken, though she kept her expression calm and her footsteps even. She'd had a lifetime to grow used to public fixation on her personal life.

To pretend it didn't bother her.

Because if she did, she'd go crazy.

Beside her the matron sent a swift sideways glance, cheeks reddening.

So Ilsa paused to admire a whimsical mural, giving the older woman time to compose herself. 'This is new. It wasn't here a month ago. It really brightens the place.'

'Yes, it does, Your Highness. The patients love it. They listed all the things they wanted included. It's good to see the young ones smile when they come out here.'

Ilsa nodded, taking in the painted scene complete

with crystal stream, fairy bower, gnomes and animals ranging from hedgehogs to unicorns. Then she noticed, in the far corner, a perfect replica of the Altbourg royal palace she knew so well. Before it stood a familiar figure wearing a coronet on her golden hair, holding the hand of a dark-haired man in the distinctive green military uniform of neighbouring Vallort.

The likenesses of herself and King Lucien were unmistakable. Despite her tension, Ilsa's lips twitched. Would the artist paint Lucien out now their engagement was over?

Except it wasn't really amusement she felt but something deeper and darker.

Not because she and Lucien had ended the betrothal foisted on them by dynastic matchmakers. But because she was tired of being reminded of it everywhere she went. Tired of being defined by her broken engagement.

Not one broken engagement but two.

One fiancé dead in a freak accident and a second spurning her to claim his waitress lover instead. Everyone saw Ilsa as a figure to be pitied.

A bubble of emotion rose and she had to work to hold it in. She longed for privacy, instead of being continually confronted by the debacle of her failed wedding plans.

Except if she stayed away from public duties people would assume she was pining for her ex-fiancé.

Plus she knew from experience that work was the best antidote to such restlessness.

Besides, the children were waiting for her. Kids whose courage in the face of often severe illness put her petty concerns in the shade. They looked forward to her visits.

She turned to the matron with a smile she knew looked serene, as if she hadn't a care in the world. 'Shall we?'

They entered a room where two teenage girls sat in hospital beds. The younger one, bald from her treatment, swept up a magazine and stuffed it behind her pillow.

She needn't have bothered. The palace media team briefed Ilsa daily. If she remembered right that one led with *Ilsa Heartbroken as Lucien Flaunts New Lover* then went on to describe her as *tragic and lonely.*

Sometimes she wished she didn't have such a retentive memory.

By the time she got home Ilsa ached with tiredness.

Smiling continually and being the perfect, composed royal took a toll when you hadn't had enough sleep.

And when paparazzi kept screaming intrusive questions from beyond the security cordons. Between the solicitous pity of the public and the hectoring barbs of the press, she felt as if she'd managed fourteen public engagements today instead of four.

She thanked the footman who opened the door to the royal family's private wing in the palace. As soon as the door shut behind her she rolled her shoulders, took off her slingback shoes and flexed her stockinged toes.

A long soak in the bath would help unknot the kinks of tension and ease her shredded nerves.

A silent laugh escaped at the idea. Princesses didn't have nerves. That luxury wasn't permitted.

As she headed down the wide corridor towards her apartment, she heard voices through the open door of the King's study. The sound of her name stopped her.

'Do you really think it's a good idea, Peter?' asked her mother. 'Ilsa's twenty-seven, not seventeen. Taking her away then was sensible, but to do it now—'

'Of course it's sensible. That time it was only her fantasies about romantic love at risk. This time the attention she's attracting is hurting Altbourg. Everything's up in the air. The strained relationship with Vallort. The end of the treaty negotiations.'

Ilsa sucked in her breath as shock punched her stomach. Her skin turned clammy.

Her father saw her as a *liability* to Altbourg?

She'd always worked hard to serve her country. She hadn't cavilled at a dynastic betrothal to Prince Justin or, when he died, to his successor, Lucien. Even though the matter-of-fact negotiations had made her feel like a second-hand car being offered to a bargain-hunter. She'd swallowed her pride, just as she'd once buried her romantic dreams and done what was demanded of her.

As for public speculation, she was doing her best to squash it, going about her royal appointments when she'd rather not see anyone.

'Peter! You can't mean it. Ilsa loves her country. No one works harder for Altbourg. She's always done everything we asked of her.'

Warmth flickered behind Ilsa's breastbone and she

found herself pressing her palm there. Her mother, at least, understood.

'Of course she does. She was trained to.' Ilsa swallowed hard, forcing down the knot of bitterness closing her throat. Her dad loved her, she knew he did, but she also knew that tone. He was in royal mode and that trumped family feeling. 'But at the moment she's a liability. Things would be easier without her here for now.'

She drew a shuddering breath that didn't fill her lungs.

So much for loyalty and obedience. For never putting her own wishes first.

At seventeen she'd believed love would transform her life. She'd been wrong, of course, but learned you didn't die of a broken heart. She'd emerged stronger and more determined. She'd found solace in duty, the love of her family and the respect of her people.

Except now her people pitied her, strangers asked the most intrusive, salacious questions and her family...

She blinked. No need to dwell on that.

What mattered, she realised, was that she'd spent her life doing what was expected of her. Doing the right thing.

Reliable Ilsa. The caring Princess who softened the face of royalty in Altbourg and fed the popular craving for a photogenic face.

But she was more than a face to be photographed for the voracious magazines. More than a hostess or gracious ambassador or even a dynastic pawn.

All her life her future had been mapped out and now,

abruptly, that map had disintegrated, leaving her rudderless and, if her father were right, a liability.

How long since she'd been simply Ilsa? Since she'd done something for herself?

Maybe that was why Ilsa had felt restless for so long. No, worse than restless. She felt hollow inside. As if all that existed was a shell with no substance.

Ilsa had been trained to be independent. She knew no one else could make her feel better. It was something she had to do herself.

Suddenly, selfishly, she *wanted* to feel better, wanted to feel something other than responsible and dutiful, if only for a short time.

She wanted a taste of freedom.

She *needed* it.

CHAPTER ONE

Noah nodded as the guy beside him elaborated on his business idea.

It wasn't the right time or place. The glamorous Monaco Yacht Club was crowded, and the band's music carried out to the massive deck through the open doors. But Noah understood the need to grab every chance to interest potential sponsors when you were starting out. Besides, the idea had merit.

Yet his attention kept straying to the dance floor.

It was filled with beautiful people, or people rich enough to pretend they were beautiful. The older ones danced circumspectly; the younger ones were obviously conscious of how they looked. Time and again he caught female eyes on him as dancers checked whether he was checking them out.

Only one stood out.

Like the others she was privileged and easy on the eye. But she seemed totally absorbed in the music, uncaring of who was watching. Her body moved to the beat in a way that dragged his gaze back again and again.

It wasn't just her absorption and apparent disinterest in the A-list crowd that set her apart.

In a short glittery dress of cobalt blue, her lips red and her gilt hair flying loose around her shoulders, she was Temptation incarnate.

Just watching her sinuous movements made his body heavy and tight with hunger.

Noah hadn't been able to get her out of his head since yesterday, when he'd deliberately kept his distance.

Ilsa of Altbourg, the alpine kingdom renowned for its ski fields, banking, robotics and quaint royal traditions.

Princess Ilsa.

Noah often dated rich women. He was a billionaire now and met his fair share. But he had a deep-seated prejudice against snobby ones who believed inherited privilege made them superior. Surely a princess would be one of those.

Yet at the charity lunch yesterday he'd wondered.

She'd been chic, composed and gracious, all the things you expected of a royal. Beautiful too, if you liked blonde snow queens. But something else had snagged his interest. Her aura of calm seemed, somehow, fragile.

Which was nonsense. She was at ease with the entitled crowd, confident and able, graciously agreeing to step in at the last minute to conduct the charity auction when the MC was taken ill.

Yet instinct told him she was more than a gilded royal.

He'd spent the lunch watching her, captivated despite himself.

Interestingly, Princess Ilsa had watched him too, though she tried to hide it. Again and again their gazes had met across the room. Each time he'd felt something ghost down his spine. A primal awareness that dragged at his belly, and lower.

Yet her glances hadn't been flirtatious.

She'd been…controlled. Contained. While those around her had grown louder and more laidback as the champagne circulated, Ilsa of Altbourg was as serenely composed at the end of the afternoon as at the beginning.

Tonight she wasn't composed. Noah watched her long, pale gold hair swish around her shoulders as she moved and felt everything in him tighten. His blood pounded a primitive beat that had nothing to do with the music and everything to do with *her*.

The woman who didn't even notice him.

A woman who should definitely not be his type.

'Mr Carson? If you could spare just half an hour somewhere quiet, I could explain properly. With some start-up funds I could—'

Noah swung round. 'I *am* interested in hearing more.' Just not now. 'Email a full proposal this week and I'll have staff look out for your message.' Then, nodding at the other's effusive thanks, he headed inside.

Noah Carson wasn't a man to ignore gut instinct.

It was time to meet the woman who'd haunted his thoughts for the last day and a half.

He was watching her. She felt it like the track of a laser across her bare arms and legs and even through the fabric of her dress, making her nipples peak and her flesh tingle.

She'd slitted open her eyes a minute ago, registering the strange frisson shivering across her skin, and glimpsed him in the distance. The broad-shouldered man with the enigmatic stare from yesterday.

She'd deliberately not asked her lunch companions about him because she didn't want to know. Yet her eyes had sought his time and again.

The music stopped and Ilsa's hair swirled into stillness around her shoulders as she dragged in deep breaths.

Her brief, precious interlude, losing herself in the mindless throb of music, was over. Time to return to the real world. Even if she *felt* different. Maybe it was just from wearing her hair down and a dress that ended halfway up her thighs. She tried to imagine her father's face if he could see her, then wiped the thought from her mind.

'Dance with me?' The dark voice, low and rich, curled around her like a silken rope, drawing her lungs tight.

Slowly Ilsa turned, knowing who she'd see.

His voice made goose bumps skitter across her skin and heat flare low in her body. Impossibly, that voice sounded familiar, as if she'd heard it before.

In her dreams maybe.

Despite her high heels her eyes were only level with his mouth.

The shock of her up-close view ricocheted through her. A tanned, squared jaw was saved from being too aggressively masculine by the hint of a cleft on his chin. And by his wide sensual mouth, curling at the corners and making her lungs squeeze even harder.

A voice in her head urged her to flee, screaming *Danger!*

But another voice whispered *Yes!*

Ilsa lifted her chin and met the most extraordinary stare she'd ever seen.

Under coal-black brows and long lashes, his eyes were turquoise. Not blue nor green but somewhere between. Clear eyes, bright and assessing.

No wonder the women on the other side of the lunch venue yesterday had preened and tittered, trying to catch his attention. Up close he was gorgeous, not merely charismatic.

'Your Highness?'

Disappointment furred her tongue and she swallowed.

For a brief second she'd imagined them yanked together by the implacable force she felt vibrating between them. By a deep, inexplicable compulsion.

Of course it was no such thing. He knew who she was. He wanted to dance with a royal. Maybe make a social or business connection and be able to name-drop later.

Ilsa pulled on a princess smile, cool and charming. 'I'm afraid you're too late. The set has ended and I—'

Music rippled on the night air. Not an upbeat pop tune like the band had just played but something slower, melodic and soulful. The lights dimmed and his straight, inky eyebrows rose just a fraction, the grooves around his mouth carving deeper in a look of complacency.

It hit her like a bolt from the blue. He'd arranged it. The change of music. The lighting.

To dance with her.

Ilsa's eyes widened and she read confirmation in his gaze. Not smugness but a level of calm self-assurance that was powerfully appealing.

She breathed deep, telling herself he was just another man wanting an introduction to royalty. But that slow inhale brought a scent that scattered her thoughts, something rich and earthy that made her nostrils flare and hormones spark.

She could say she was leaving. Or that she'd had enough dancing for one night.

Instead she nodded and was rewarded with a flare of what looked like anticipation in those stunning eyes, even as his mouth firmed into a straight line.

As if he too wasn't sure this was a good idea.

Then he took her hand in his and slid his other arm around her, his palm sitting at her waist, all perfectly respectable.

It didn't feel respectable as he led her into a slow dance. Ilsa's nerves jumped and jangled as if she'd touched an electric wire and her breathing turned shallow.

By contrast, she moved in his arms as if they'd danced together for years. As if their bodies knew each other, anticipating every move, every shift of weight and slight pressure of hands.

Still their eyes held, and it felt impossibly intimate.

Which proved how unexciting her life had been.

Then his attention dropped to her lips and heat seared her. It took a second to realise he was watching her tongue trace her suddenly dry mouth.

Did he think she was trying to entice him? Dismay unfurled and she stiffened.

'Easy, Princess.'

He firmed his hold as she bumped into someone behind her. Now he held her closer, near enough that she felt his body heat radiating into her.

He moved with easy grace and she wondered what he did professionally. Sportsman? He had the power and athleticism and, she felt sure, enough single-minded determination. But his air of authority suggested something else. As did the calculation in his eyes, as if he assessed her just as thoroughly as she assessed him.

She was torn between wanting to know everything about him and knowing that when she did this fantasy of an elemental connection between them would shatter.

Was it crazy to hang onto the illusion a little longer?

'Why did you ask me to dance?' she asked finally.

He didn't answer immediately and when he did she wasn't prepared. 'Because I couldn't not.'

That jolted her right to the marrow of her bones.

There was no humour in his expression, just an intense focus that pierced several defensive layers. In other circumstances she'd expect some facile compliment about her looks. Instead his stare transfixed her. Just as well her body was working on autopilot, swaying to the seductive music in perfect time with his.

They were surrounded by people, hemmed in by dancers, yet everything beyond the pair of them was distant, as if they existed in a bubble, cut off from the world.

Ilsa blinked, realising her hand had crept from his

shoulder to his hard chest, planted there as if staking a claim. Heat flushed her cheeks and she started to move her hand back when he shook his head. 'Leave it.'

She didn't take orders from any man, apart from her King, but the gravel note in those terse words made her pause.

'Why?' she asked again. 'Why couldn't you *not* ask me to dance?'

His mouth twisted up in a smile that she felt deep in some vital organ. 'I planned not to. I saw you yesterday and didn't approach you.'

Ilsa nodded. She'd told herself she was glad he hadn't. That he clearly wasn't as interested in her as she was in him. But he'd been on her mind ever since.

That was a first for her. Since her ill-fated teenage romance she hadn't fretted over any man. Yet ever since yesterday's lunch she'd wondered if she'd see him again. Monaco was tiny after all.

'But I couldn't ignore *this*.' He captured her hand, lifted it from his chest and skimmed his lips across her fingers.

The instant jolt of sensation buckled her knees and he tightened his embrace to support her. Ilsa's eyes felt like saucers as she met his knowing stare.

'You feel it too.' Yet he didn't look triumphant. If anything, his features looked stern. As if…

'You don't like me.' The words shot out before she could think about them. But tonight, with him, her usual caution had been stripped away.

'I don't know you.'

Ilsa was used to people eager to meet her and spend

time with her. It was strange to feel she had to earn his approval, that he might even be predisposed not to approve.

But she wanted him to.

She turned her hand in his and stroked a finger down his palm, feeling him shudder and watching his eyelids droop in an expression of pure sexual desire.

Low in her pelvis she felt a new sensation. Something that made her shift her weight, trying to ease… not pain, but a sort of throbbing tenderness.

Ilsa snagged a deep breath, abruptly conscious that they'd stopped moving on the edge of the dance floor, while other couples passed them.

She should step back, put distance between them.

But this feeling, this man, were too extraordinary.

If she turned away she knew she'd regret it. This flash of connection was rare. Would she ever experience it again? Instinct said no. Especially not with some appropriate suitor arranged by her father.

'I don't know you either.'

'That's easily remedied.' He paused. 'Come with me and we'll get to know each other.'

His words hung between them, inviting, tempting. Full of innuendo.

The intensity of his scrutiny stole Ilsa's breath. Or maybe it was the effect of standing so close to him, locked in his embrace.

The idea was outrageous. To go out into the night with a man she didn't know. It went against every rule.

Ilsa had lived her life by the rule book.

In her peripheral vision she saw the curious looks

they were attracting. They couldn't stay like this indefinitely. They had to move.

Yet she couldn't bring herself to care. She was tired of worrying about image and public perception.

'Who are you?' Amazing to be considering this yet not know his name.

'Noah. Noah Carson.'

The name was familiar. Anyone who read the international press would recognise it. A self-made multi-billionaire known for innovation, dazzling success and the glamorous women in his life. Now she realised it was a hint of an Australian accent she heard in his deep voice.

He read her expression. 'You know the name?'

'You're notorious.'

His mouth turned down. 'Do you believe everything you read in the press?'

Despite herself, she flinched. It was a sore point given the flights of fancy that had been published about her ever since she hit puberty, and now the pity, scorn and lewd speculation levelled at her and Lucien.

She saw Noah register her reaction. 'Absolutely not. Do you?'

Was that why he gave the impression he responded to her against his better judgement? Maybe he saw her as leeching off her people and giving nothing back.

'No.'

He squeezed her hand and her thoughts scattered as pleasure rippled across her skin and into her bloodstream.

Noah leaned forward, his words a whisper across her temple. 'You're safe with me, Princess. You have

The implacable conclusion sent icy shivers coursing through her. In that moment she regretted every moment of weakness. Regretted feeling bad for invoking that hint of disappointment in his eyes.

She had nothing to be ashamed of. Not when vanquishing her and her family was his sole, true purpose.

She snatched his shirt from her shoulders, crushing her body's instant insistence on its warmth as she tossed it back to him. "You should know by now that threats don't faze me. We're still here, still standing after all you and your family have done. So go ahead, do your worst."

Head held high, she whirled away from him. She made it only three steps before he captured her wrist. She spun around, intent on pushing him away.

But that ruthlessness was coupled with something else. Something hot and blazing and all-consuming in his eyes.

She belatedly read it as lust before he was tugging her closer, wrapping one hand around her waist and the other in her hair. "This stubborn determination is admirable. Hell, I'd go so far as to say it's a turn-on, because God knows I admire strong, willful women," he muttered, his lips a hairsbreadth from hers, "but fiery passion will only get you so far."

"And what are you going to do about it?" she taunted a little too breathlessly. Every cell in her body traitorously strained toward him, yearning for things she knew she shouldn't want but desperately needed anyway.

He froze, then with a strangled sound leaving his throat, he slammed his lips onto hers.

He kissed her like he was starved for it. *For her.*

Why, Amelie wonders, does she feel such a wild attraction to Atu? He wants to buy her family's beach resort, so he's completely off-limits. Yet surrendering to their heat was inevitable...and now she's pregnant with his heir!

Read on for a sneak preview of
Maya Blake's next story for Harlequin Presents
Bound by Her Rival's Baby

A breeze washed over Amelie and she shivered.

Within one moment and the next, Atu was shrugging off his shirt.

"Wh-what are you doing?" she blurted as he came toward her.

Another mirthless twist of his lips. "You may deem me an enemy, but I don't want you catching cold and falling ill. Or worse."

She aimed a glare his way. "Not until I've signed on whatever dotted line you're determined to foist on me, you mean?"

That look of fury returned. This time accompanied by a flash of disappointment. As if he had the right to such a lofty emotion where she was concerned. She wanted, no, *needed* to refuse this small offer of comfort.

To return to her room and come up with a definite plan that removed him from her life for good.

So why was she drawing the flaps of his shirt closer? Her fingers clinging to the warm cotton as if she'd never let it go?

She must have made a sound at the back of her throat, because his head swung toward her, his eyes holding hers for an age before he exhaled harshly.

His lips firmed and for a long stretch he didn't speak. "You need to accept that I'm the best bet you have right now. There's no use fighting. I'm going to win eventually. How soon depends entirely on you."

CHAPTER TWO

ILSA WAS CONSCIOUS of the stir they made, leaving the crowded party, and was pleased Noah didn't stop to exchange greetings with the people eager to catch their attention.

She was grateful for the clasp of his hand. His touch reassured as a flurry of nerves hit out of nowhere.

Going back to a man's place, any man's place, to *get to know him better*, was uncharted territory. Yet walking beside him felt nothing but right. She was aware of his easy stride, curtailed, she was sure, to cater for her shorter steps, the brush of his sleeve against her bare arm and the heat of his tall frame.

As they left the building she caught sight of a familiar bull-necked figure and implacable face. The guard her father had sent after her.

No doubt before the night was out her father would hear where she'd gone and with whom.

'Are you okay?' Noah stopped, turning to face her. 'Have you changed your mind?'

The tilt of his head spoke of concern, even if his grasp of her fingers spoke of urgency. Ilsa liked that he'd

noticed her momentary distraction and asked that all-important question.

She leaned close, breathing in the deep, aromatic notes of his male scent. 'I'm good. I haven't changed my mind.'

White teeth gleamed against his tan as he grinned and Ilsa had trouble catching her breath. The man was hot, sexy *and* caring.

'Excellent. It's not far.'

Not far turned out to be at the far end of the marina.

Instead of a towering, ostentatious super cruiser, Noah's was a classic vintage yacht, all beautiful lines in sleek white and teak and large enough to have been used for round-the-world royal cruises.

'Your yacht's beautiful.'

Ilsa paused to take it in. You could tell a lot about a man from how he spent his money. If she read Noah right, he appreciated fine craftsmanship and quality as well as luxury. She knew wealthy men devoted to out-doing their rivals with the biggest, flashiest cruiser, jet or car. Noah clearly didn't feel the need to prove him-self that way.

Another knot inside her frayed and disintegrated. Surely a man who took the time to appreciate substance and quality was the sort who'd take time to ensure they both enjoyed tonight to the full? A patient man.

It was the closest she'd come to feeling nervous about what was going to happen between them.

'She's not new. But I'm a firm believer in recycling.'

Was that an edge to his voice? She couldn't read his expression from his profile.

'New isn't always better,' Ilsa replied. 'Besides, she's got character.' Even Ilsa, who was no expert on yachts, saw that.

He swung round, his eyes meeting hers, and Ilsa had the impression she'd surprised him. He lifted their linked hands and brushed a kiss across her knuckles.

Desire hit her like a wave, crashing through her and eddying into every part of her body.

'Shall we?' he murmured.

Her smile threatened to undo him. It was full of delight and anticipation, making his own expectations ratchet up to impossible levels.

Noah told himself he was doomed to disappointment. Reality couldn't live up to the incredible build-up.

Nevertheless, he wanted to rush her aboard. He had to remind himself not to jump her the moment their feet hit the deck. They had all night and he'd take his time. Especially as, despite her smile, those smoky blue eyes held a hint of trepidation.

Could it be that Ilsa, the confident, poised Princess with the world at her feet, was nervous?

'Just a second.'

She slipped her hand from his and immediately he felt the loss, his fingers clenching into a fist.

When was the last time he'd held hands with a woman? With Ilsa it felt as natural as breathing.

She bent to take off her shoes then straightened, dangling the sexy stilettos from her fingers. 'They're not good for the deck, are they?'

Noah captured her hand and led her forward. Right

now he didn't give a damn about pockmarks on the wood. But he liked her thoughtfulness.

Once aboard he paused, remembering his resolve to take his time. Maybe he'd imagined her momentary nerves, but a slight delay would only make the final consummation more delicious.

Instead of taking her straight to the master suite he led her to the spacious lounge. A few lamps were on, bathing the room in an intimate golden glow.

'What's your favourite drink?' he asked.

'Cherry juice,' she said instantly, then looked as surprised as he felt. Quickly she turned to survey the room, making him wonder if she was covering embarrassment. 'Altbourg is renowned for its cherries so it's a staple for pies, strudels—'

'And juice.'

She nodded. 'But I know you're unlikely to have it. Apple juice would be good, thanks. Or sparkling water.'

Noah had expected her to ask for champagne or some exotic cocktail. Was he in danger of typecasting? Bitter experience had taught him socialites were predictable.

Reluctantly he released her hand and went to the bar, his body already tight with arousal.

'You're right, no cherry juice. But we've got sparkling water.'

When he'd poured them both glasses he turned to find her standing where he'd left her. The only difference was that her shoes were placed neatly on the floor and she held one hand across her abdomen. It fell to her side as he offered her a glass. Was that another hint of nervousness? Surely that was unlikely.

'Is it too cool for you outside? The view's good.'

Because if they stayed in here he wouldn't be able to resist sitting beside her on the lounge. Within two minutes his hand would be up that short skirt and the other hauling down her zip, even though he'd promised himself he'd give her a little time to adjust.

Hard and urgent would be fantastic, but he wanted a second, third and fourth time with Ilsa. Which meant curbing his lust to give at least the impression that he was a civilised man.

'Outside is fine.' She took a sip from her glass. 'If I get cold I'll let you know.'

Then he could warm her, preferably with full body to body contact. Noah repressed a sigh. *Soon…*

They sat looking across the harbour at the lights of the city. The sound of the yacht club party floated across the water but here in the velvety darkness, sheltered from prying eyes, it felt like they were cocooned in another world. The same feeling had hit him yesterday when their gazes had locked across the room. And again tonight.

He shook off the fantasy and turned to the woman beside him.

'We don't know each other except for this.' Noah reached out and her soft hand slid unhesitatingly into his. Instantly his body responded, relaxing as if in relief at the same time as his flesh pulled tight in arousal. He swallowed, surprised all over again at the potency of this awareness. 'I suggest we take a little time to… explore each other.'

That didn't come out the way he'd intended, but his

brain was being hijacked by a hormonal flood. Thinking of anything but sex took effort. Yet he sensed the need to take time with Ilsa. She was eager yet surprisingly diffident. He was determined not to scare her off.

'You want to know about me?' Was she surprised?

'And vice versa.'

She hesitated. 'How about twenty questions? We each take turns answering.'

Noah stroked his thumb across her wrist and felt her pulse leap. His own hammered like a piston, just from being so close to her. 'Not twenty.' He didn't have that much patience. 'Let's leave some for later.'

Her soft chuckle was a caress, teasing his senses.

Was there anything he didn't like about her?

Despite his caution around women who saw themselves as a cut above the rest of society, Ilsa kept surprising him.

'Okay. Tell me, Noah…' She paused on his name and he wondered if she enjoyed saying it. It was the first time he'd heard it on her lips and he liked her sudden huskiness. 'Something you've done recently that made you happy.'

He took a drink while he considered. Beside him Ilsa put her glass down, shifted in her seat and rested her palm on her stomach.

He thought of the fantastic deal he'd just made with a consortium of French companies. That had made him smile. Then he remembered laughing out loud just two days ago when his brother's family had visited him here.

'Easy. Spending time with my nephew. He's thirteen

and full of energy. Let him near a windsurfer or pad-
dleboard, or give him a chance to beat me at his new
computer game and he's happy.'

'It sounds like you get on well.'

'We're similar types. Lots of energy and drive.' He
paused. 'So, Ilsa, why are you here in Monaco?'

It was hard to tell in the dark but, holding her hand,
he sensed her tension.

'The simple answer or the complicated one?' she
said eventually.

'Both.'

'That counts as two questions.'

She shifted as if getting more comfortable and he
caught a hint of the scent that had tantalised him as
they danced. Light and citrusy. His breath quickened.

'So be it.' The sooner they finished the sooner they'd
be naked together.

'The simple answer is that paparazzi can't operate
in Monaco.'

'Ah.' Maybe he was wrong. Maybe what he'd thought
on the dock to be nerves was just the wariness of a
woman expecting to be spied on wherever she went.
He'd looked her up online yesterday and knew she'd
been targeted by the paparazzi recently. He felt sorry
for her. And curious about the truth of what had happened between her and her two ex-fiancés.

'And the complicated answer?'

Her fingers twitched in his hold and he was acutely
conscious of the slow breath she drew in, her breasts
rising tantalisingly in his peripheral vision. Noah sti-
fled the need to turn and survey her. Maybe the dark-

ness and freedom from scrutiny would encourage her to share more.

He guessed she found it challenging, sharing something personal. Noah understood that. He was the same. Yet he felt tonight as if the usual barriers had come down.

'What's said aboard stays aboard, Ilsa. I don't break confidences, just as I don't expect you to break mine. But I don't want you uncomfortable. If I've asked something too private...' Even if he wanted to know everything about her. 'We can—'

'No, it's fine. I'm just not sure I can put it into words. Though it might be good to talk about it.'

She threaded her fingers through his and Noah basked in her willingness to trust him. It was amazing how important that felt.

'You probably know about my broken engagement.'

He turned his head, catching the glint of her bright eyes in the gloom.

'I heard you'd called off your wedding.'

'Thank you.' She swung round to face him fully and even in the dark he felt a slam of heat as her eyes met his.

'What for?'

'Acknowledging I was involved in the decision. I should be used to the press by now, but I'm sick of being painted as some pathetic victim whom Lucien wronged! It was a joint decision and we were both relieved when it was over.'

Interesting. So she wasn't longing for her ex-fiancé. But what about his cousin, who'd been King before

Lucien? Ilsa had been engaged to him until his sudden death in a road accident. Did she carry a torch for him?

Noah frowned, his hold tightening on her hand. She was free now but he didn't like the idea of her yearning for some lost love. He wanted her attention on him!

Ego, Carson. She only met you tonight.

Yet logic didn't come into this. It was amazing how proprietorial he felt about this woman. How inevitable it felt touching her, knowing that soon now they'd be naked together.

Again she shifted in her seat, making him wonder if she were uncomfortable or simply edgy. 'You could say my life, and the plans made for me, have unravelled.'

Plans made *for* her? Not *by* her?

'I thought taking up the reins of my usual life would see me through all the fuss and bother. If I kept busy, did my bit for the country, not just with the public events but my other projects, things would blow over and I'd feel…' She paused, making him forget to ponder what her projects might be and wonder instead about her feelings.

'The fact is…' she said with a brittle laugh that raked his spine like nails down a blackboard. 'The fact is I'm not needed in Altbourg at the moment.' She paused and he heard her swallow. 'And I wasn't settling into my old routine. So I thought a little time away was in order.'

'Some R and R. Well, you've come to the right place.' Noah's confident tone hid his sympathy at her vulnerability. She hadn't given details but her voice…

'That's right. It will be perfect for me.'

She sounded so bright and determined he knew she made an effort to mask her feelings.

He remembered her dancing. She'd been absorbed, lost to the people around her, but she hadn't necessarily looked happy.

Noah stroked his finger across her wrist, feeling her pulse jump and, despite his need to know more, desire jabbed.

Sitting so close, hearing each sigh and shuffle of movement, reading her body's unconscious responses to him and trying not to stare at this woman, grew more taxing by the moment. His trousers were too snug across his groin and he knew going slow when they came together would be almost impossible. Maybe they'd manage it the second time.

'Why are you in Monte Carlo?' She yanked his thoughts back to their Q&A session.

He shrugged, stifling the urge to haul her into his arms and plant his lips on hers. If she needed this time…

'I had a deal to finalise, which I've done, and now I'm having a break. Business has been bedlam the last year or so.' Which was good, because his new initiatives were succeeding. 'I worked through a bad flu and it took me longer than it should to shake it off.' His family had been on his back to take a proper holiday. Had even flown here last week to make sure he did. Even if they'd camouflaged it as a long overdue family holiday. 'So I'm taking a few weeks to cruise the Med.'

Except now the prospect of heading off on a sailing holiday had lost its appeal. He'd rather explore Ilsa than any photogenic port.

Urgency filled him.

He needed to hold her in his arms again, properly this time.

Noah sat straighter. 'One last question each.' He felt her eyes on him as he sought to distil the hundreds of things he wanted to know about her into one that would do for now. 'What do you want from life, Ilsa? What's important to you?'

That would tell him what sort of woman she was.

She went still. To his chagrin she slid her hand free of his, leaning forward in her seat and wrapping her arms around her middle.

Instinct told him he'd just made a huge mistake.

Silently he cursed. Why hadn't he asked her favourite ice cream flavour or whether she liked sport?

'What do I want?' She paused, frowning, and he sensed it was something she hadn't considered before. Finally, after a long pause she spoke. 'I can tell you what's important. My people, my country, my family.' Her voice sounded tight and unfamiliar. 'As for what I want from life…' She shook her head and her lush mouth turned down at the corners. Noah felt a phantom jab of discomfort to his gut, seeing what looked like distress. 'That's just it. I don't know any more.'

She shot to her feet and moved away. Instinctively he followed but when he reached for her she shook her head. Ilsa stood, arms crossed, before him.

He didn't like even this small distance between them. But it was his fault. He shouldn't have probed so deep when she'd obviously had a difficult time recently. What

had he been thinking? This woman clouded his usually clear head.

'How about you, Noah? What do you want?'

That was easy. 'Good health, good friends, enough challenge in business to keep me interested, and time with my family.'

'That sounds…perfect.'

Why did she have to sound so damned wistful? It wasn't just her voice either. Noah sensed a change in her. Something was wrong. He stepped closer.

She spoke quickly. 'Could you direct me to the bathroom, please?'

Noah frowned, loath to let her out of his sight.

Then his pulse quickened as anticipation stirred. Ilsa wanted to freshen up, ready for a night making love.

CHAPTER THREE

ILSA SHOOK HER HEAD, not wanting to believe it was true, but knowing it was.

Of course it was. Her life was a disaster lately. *She* was a disaster, according to her father. She should have expected malicious fate would play another trick on her.

She dragged a comb through her hair, tugging hard, telling herself that was what made her eyes water. Not disappointment and razor-sharp frustration such as she'd never known. And plain old-fashioned pain.

Another cramp twisted through her abdomen and she braced against the bathroom basin, breathing slowly.

Some women had easy periods that turned up as regular as clockwork. Not Ilsa. She, like her mother and her cousin, had endometriosis. In her case it meant irregular cramping periods. Usually the aches started long before the bleeding but not tonight.

Tonight she'd barely had any warning.

She blinked into the mirror, eyes filling and mouth crumpling at the sheer unfairness of it. Why now? Why tonight when she'd just met *him*?

Fate definitely had it in for her.

Noah Carson was the first man she'd been really attracted to since her teens. The first man she'd wanted. And, in tonight's strange, reckless mood, she'd decided to let him be her first.

No, that was too passive. This wasn't about *letting* him be her first real lover, but acting on her bone-deep need for him. An urgent desire such as she'd never known could exist, much less between strangers.

She felt ready to risk anything for a night in his arms.

Everything had seemed so perfect, so inevitable, that any last qualms had withered when he took her hand and those unspoken messages passed between their bodies. As if, instead of being strangers, they already knew each other in the most essential ways.

Ilsa blinked, suppressing the urge to howl in outrage and despair.

She'd never experienced anything like this, and probably never would again.

Next time her father organised her betrothal for dynastic purposes, there'd be no escape. She'd marry some man out of duty. The chance she'd feel anything like what she felt for Noah was non-existent.

For years she'd accepted that as her fate. But now...

She'd changed. She craved more. She wanted...

Jerking up her chin she met over-bright eyes in the mirror.

It doesn't matter what you want. Tonight just won't happen. And Noah Carson isn't going to wait around for a week until you're ready. The fantasy is over. You've missed your chance.

Putting her comb back in her purse, Ilsa fought the

urge to rage and scream her disappointment. She pushed back her shoulders and schooled her features into a mask of calm.

When she reached the large sitting room, she found Noah waiting for her instead of on the deck.

Her heart bumped hard against her ribs then took up an unsteady beat.

With his hands in his trouser pockets, his stance accentuated his wide shoulders and lean length. He looked delicious, especially when his searing gaze took hers and his mouth curled up in a smile she felt in every pore and deeper, right at the centre of her being.

Ilsa swallowed. She had no choice but to walk away. Yet it felt like the hardest thing she'd ever done. Far harder than ending her engagement.

'Have I told you how good you look?' His words burred across her skin, drawing it tight with goose bumps. 'Absolutely delectable.'

'I—' She'd been about to respond in kind and say he looked good enough to eat. Her mind snagged on the notion of tasting her way across his body. Then snapped back to the fact that wouldn't be possible. 'I'm so sorry, Noah. But I have to leave.'

His smile disappeared. 'Did you get a message? Something urgent?'

'No.' Maybe she should have lied and said yes, but Ilsa was innately truthful. Besides, whatever it was she and Noah shared felt too visceral, too profound for lies. 'But I'm afraid this isn't going to work.'

The discomfort was worse now, a dull ache circling

to her lower back to round off the tight, sharp fist of pain low in her abdomen.

Ilsa sucked in her breath and stood straighter, fighting the urge to hunch over.

'I don't understand.' Something flickered in his eyes that she couldn't read. 'Is it something I said?'

'No, nothing like that.' If anything, she liked him even more following his disclosures. How could she *not* be drawn to a man who got his kicks out of time with his nephew? Whose life goal wasn't making money, but enjoying family and the rewards that came from challenging himself?

He stepped nearer, tugging his hands free, and again the air between them snapped and sizzled with awareness.

Ilsa wanted to snuggle close, ask if he'd stay in port until she was over this inconvenience. But that was asking too much. Besides, she didn't want to blurt out the humdrum reason she couldn't be his lover. Maybe it was pride or prudishness, but this felt too personal to disclose. She'd rather he remembered her as alluring and mysterious.

'It's your prerogative to change your mind, but at least tell me why.'

His gaze bored into hers and she felt it right down to her bones. He was right. He deserved an explanation.

Ilsa was a naturally private person and her royal training had accentuated that tendency. But she had already shared so much, things she'd never imagined sharing with a stranger.

Besides, Noah didn't feel like a stranger.

She drew a slow breath and shrugged. 'My period has started and I'll be spending the night curled up with a hot-water bottle to battle stomach cramps.'

Noah stared, stunned, into her lovely face. Despite her attempt at a wry smile, he read distress in her too-bright eyes. And—he saw it now—pain in the pinch of her nostrils and the pucker of her forehead.

Then her shoulders hunched on a silent gasp and her hand went to her belly, as it had through their game of question and answer.

'Why didn't you tell me straight away?' Her apparent rejection had made him wonder if he'd misjudged her. If she might be another privileged woman who liked to play games.

She shook her head. 'It's not something I usually discuss.'

He heard it in her voice now too. She was breathing through pain and he hated that.

'What can I do?'

Misty blue eyes met his, startled. 'Nothing. I've taken something for the pain. I just have to ride it out till the medication starts working.'

Meanwhile she looked in no fit state to return to her hotel. Her brow looked damp and to his dismay he realised she was shivering.

Noah moved swiftly, lifting her into his arms before she had a chance to do more than gasp, then marching to a nearby sofa.

'What are you doing?'

Her shoes thudded to the floor as she grabbed hold of

him. Noah sat down, cradling her across his lap, trying not to think about how perfectly she fitted his embrace and how his body clamoured for hers.

He looked at the sexy shoes tumbled on the floor rather than the sexy woman in his arms and worked on stifling his physical response. It was harder than he'd imagined, but nor did he like to imagine watching her walk away from him, especially when she was in pain.

'You're hurting.' He cradled her closer, leaning back so she tipped towards his body. 'And I'm comforting you. I don't know anything about period pain but I remember breaking a bone as a kid and waiting for the painkillers to kick in. My mum held me in her arms and it helped.'

She didn't say anything but after a moment he felt her shudder.

Was she getting worse? He tilted his head to see her face and discovered her crystal-bright eyes welling, her mouth a crooked line.

Something in his chest tumbled hard against his ribs. 'Ilsa? Is the pain worse? Do you need a doctor?'

She shook her head and a strand of light gold hair slipped across her bare shoulder. He watched her slender throat work then she blinked, clearing her eyes and offering a ghost of a smile.

Heat exploded inside him. Strangely he'd swear it had nothing to do with sex or the feel of her soft body against his. But everything to do with her smile and that sense of connection, just like when they'd sat side by side on the darkened deck, sharing confidences.

'You're right,' she said eventually, her suddenly

husky voice catching at something inside him. 'Being held helps. I've never...' She paused. 'Thank you, Noah.'

Never what? He didn't push. She had enough going on without his curiosity.

So he shifted his weight to get more comfortable and reassured her when she protested that she was too heavy.

Eventually they lapsed into silence. Noah pondered his unprecedented response to this woman as she nestled against him, her head below his chin. Three hours ago he couldn't have imagined his evening ending like this. But then three hours ago he hadn't done more than lust after Ilsa from a distance.

The real woman, close up, was at once more complex and confusing, and far more appealing than he'd imagined. More appealing than any other he'd known.

The part of him that foresaw problems and worked out ways to avoid them warned that Ilsa could disrupt his life, just when he had things going the way he liked.

But a still deeper part of his psyche wanted her on any terms. She'd attracted him on the dance floor. Intrigued him when she asked for juice instead of champagne. Surprised him when she asked what made him smile and what he wanted from life, then moved him when she grew flustered when she couldn't easily answer that herself.

And through it all desire throbbed hot and strong.

She engaged his mind and his heart as well as his body. It was an intoxicating combination.

'How long is your holiday?' he asked abruptly. 'Days? Weeks?'

She tilted her head back against his shoulder. 'I don't have firm plans. I left on the spur of the moment.'

If her schedule was anything like that of the other royals he'd met, that was some feat. Even the quick research he'd done on her last night revealed a woman with a heavy public and diplomatic schedule, more so even than her brother's, the heir to the throne.

He looked down at her and felt the tightness in his belly ease.

Noah smiled and watched, mesmerised, as her pupils dilated. Whatever this was between them, he wanted it. And so did she. His time was his own for the next several weeks and, by her own admission, Ilsa wasn't in a rush to return home.

An idea had come to him that made his skin tingle, in a good way. As it did when he got his best ideas. It would mean taking a chance, but instinct urged that it was a chance he must take.

His smile widened. 'Why not spend your holiday with me? Let's sail the Mediterranean together.'

Ilsa gaped up into his calm, confident face and told herself she'd misheard.

But how could she have? She was curled against him like a kid needing comfort—something she'd feel embarrassed about in the cold, hard light of day—and watched his mouth form the words. And, despite his smile, she didn't read levity in his expression.

'You're serious.' It didn't seem possible.

'Absolutely.'

If she had more energy, Ilsa would have catapulted

out of his hold and found a spot elsewhere in the room, where the cocoon of warmth enfolding her, and the firm cushion of his body, wouldn't distract her.

But there was no way Ilsa would give up his embrace until she had to. She couldn't recall the last time she'd been comforted like this and it really did help. Her mother had cuddled her close when she arrived home after ending her engagement, but that had lasted only a few moments, since Ilsa's father had been there too, waiting impatiently to discuss the political ramifications of the scandal.

Apart from that it had been years since she'd felt the comfort of a physical embrace. She didn't count circling the royal ballroom, held close, but not too close, by various dance partners.

'But you want…' She frowned and shut her mouth before she blurted out the obvious.

'You. Yes, I do.' Was it his deep, firm voice saying he wanted her that shot a bolt of longing through her? Or the way his nostrils flared as if drawing in her scent? He dipped his head, as if needing to get closer, and Ilsa's lips parted in anticipation. But he didn't lean in to press his lips to hers.

Her pulse thundered as she imagined Noah's kiss. Even as they'd sat in the dark, holding hands, talking as freely as only two strangers could, she'd been thinking of his mouth on hers.

'I want you, Ilsa.' His words were so potent they seared into her, making her shiver. Already he had a powerful effect on her, but hearing him say it in that

suddenly rough voice was unlike anything she'd ever known. 'But you need time.'

'You'd give me that time?' It didn't seem credible. Everything between them had been so immediate, so blatant and urgent. Surely this was a man used to getting what he wanted instantly. 'I'm not talking about a day or two, you know.'

A glimmer of a smile lit his intent features and Ilsa felt it like the tug of a thread, pulled tight within her. 'I admit I'm no expert on the female cycle, but even I know that.'

Finally Ilsa gathered the energy to move, to sit straight, albeit on his lap, with his arms loose around her. It was appalling how at home she felt there. Even the sharp ache in her abdomen seemed more bearable when she was tucked up against him.

The realisation pleased yet at the same time worried her. As if she'd relinquished something to this man she barely knew.

'Why, Noah? Why me? And why go to such lengths?'

It wasn't distrust she felt, but confusion. She wasn't a woman for whom men made spectacular, dramatic gestures. She'd never been invited to a sybaritic idyll. She *hoped* that was what he had in mind.

'Why you?' He shook his head. 'I don't know. Either it's too complex to explain or so simple it doesn't need explanation. But you feel it too, don't you, Ilsa? This bond, this attraction.'

'I feel…something.' There spoke cautious Ilsa, the woman who'd been trained to guard every word and look.

Suddenly she despised that woman, living her life

by the rule book, always concerned for what others thought. For once in her life she wanted to be impulsive and utterly selfish. She wanted to feel all the glorious things Noah stirred in her and much, much more.

'Yes,' she said, her voice louder, decisive. 'I feel like something's got into my bloodstream and when we touch it sizzles. But it makes me feel at peace too.' As if such contrary feelings could coexist!

It felt liberating to admit the truth, no matter how outlandish.

'You *do* feel it.' He met her stare with a smile and her heart lifted.

She wasn't alone then. If this was some strange illusion, at least it was shared. Noah Carson had no reason to lie.

'What if we wake up tomorrow or the next day and it's gone?' she asked. 'No sizzle left?'

His serious look turned into a slow smile that threatened to melt her bones. 'That doesn't mean we can't enjoy each other's company. If you get tired of me we'll put into port and you can fly home.'

Home. The word brought no solace. For the last couple of years she'd assumed her home would be Vallort where she'd be Queen, wife of a man she didn't love but whom she respected. Beyond that, home was Altbourg where she'd been born, but that wasn't the place for her now. She was a liability there.

'Ilsa?' Gently he tilted her head back, brushing her hair from her face. She softened, leaning into his touch.

'It's a mad idea.'

'Not mad at all. Following your instincts is never a mistake.'

He spoke with such certainty she almost believed him. She *did* believe him. Not enough to think there'd be no regrets. But Ilsa was tired of living a half-life, hemmed in by caution and others' expectations. She wanted to follow her passions. To live. To take a chance.

She thought of the reports painting her as a tragic victim and the malicious jibes against Lucien's poor lover.

Swanning around the Mediterranean with Noah would give the press something else to chew on, and maybe take some of the heat off Lucien and Aurélie. Her father would have a fit but right now she couldn't bring herself to care.

If the press got wind of it there would be a new sort of scandal and she wouldn't be viewed as *poor innocent Ilsa* any more. She doubted even her clever father would be able to organise an arranged royal marriage for her then. That alone was a good reason to say *yes*.

But that wasn't why she wanted to agree.

She lifted her hand to Noah's neck, pressed her fingertips lightly to his hot flesh and wondered at how magnificent that felt. He shuddered, his eyelids drooping in a look that spoke a language as ancient as the divide between the sexes.

That stare, that shiver, made her feel powerful and desired. She opened her mouth to say *yes* when realisation hit. Elation turned to dismay.

'I can't.' Disappointment tugged her mouth down at the corners. How could she have forgotten? 'I'm guest

of honour later this week at a dinner hosted by the Monegasque royal family. I can't back out. I gave my word.'

'I see.' His hand covered hers and his look turned unreadable.

It was one thing to tell herself she was free to make her own choices now. It was another to insult her hosts so blatantly. She couldn't do it.

But that didn't lessen her disappointment.

'I have an important meeting in Athens soon and can't stay here,' Noah murmured.

So that was it. Ilsa's flutter of excitement became a crumpled feeling of sadness. She sighed, trying not to think about how devastated she felt.

'Well, I'd better—'

'Wait.' His eyes held hers. 'Tell me, if you could choose one place to holiday in the Mediterranean where would it be?'

Ilsa frowned. What was the point of asking when she couldn't go with him?

'Ilsa?'

'Turkey. I've never been to Turkey and it sounds wonderful.'

'Then meet me in Istanbul at the end of the week.'

'I…' She swallowed hard, excitement and something that felt like too much emotion clogging her throat. Noah made it sound so easy, so right that they should be together. Nothing in her life had felt easy or right for a long time.

His eyes held hers so intently she felt like she was falling into an endless warm ocean. 'Don't say no, Ilsa. Say yes, or at least that you'll think about it.'

The whole idea was outrageous. So *not* her.

The press would find out and then there'd be a scandal. But she couldn't seem to care.

'That sounds wonderful.'

CHAPTER FOUR

NEXT MORNING ILSA slept later than she had in years. She woke to familiar pain low in her body but also to a luxurious feeling of having rested well.

And fizzing anticipation.

Or was it disbelief at what she'd agreed to last night?

She lay pondering her decision to embark on an affair with Noah Carson. She'd be breaking with her past and burning her bridges. News of it would undoubtedly reach her family and the press. Given her savagely ticking biological clock and fertility problem she should be looking for a man who wanted to settle down, not a holiday fling.

Yet instead of second thoughts Ilsa felt elation. Every instinct told her she had made the right decision.

That feeling intensified when she turned on her phone and discovered a message from Noah inviting her to breakfast, brunch or lunch, depending on when she woke. Ilsa grinned as she texted back.

Excitement thrilled down her spine. Instead of a morning curled up with a book and a heat pack, she'd see Noah.

The man who would be her first lover.

* * *

'You look scrumptious,' Noah bent his head and murmured near her ear as he ushered her across the sumptuous lobby and out into the sunshine.

Ilsa's pulse fluttered wildly and she tried to contain her delight. 'You look pretty good yourself.'

That was a huge understatement. In casual jeans and a pale green shirt Noah looked rangy, sexy and utterly masculine. Her heart somersaulted at the way his eyes crinkled at the corners when he smiled at her.

'How do you feel today?' he murmured.

'Fantastic!'

That made him grin, a flash of white in his tanned face and a look in his eyes that made her knees tremble. If she didn't feel so excited she'd worry about his impact on her, but today that didn't seem to matter.

'Me too. How's the pain?'

She shrugged. 'Bearable.' She'd taken painkillers and she didn't want to talk about such mundanities. 'I thought you were sailing today.'

That surely explained her excitement at receiving his message.

Noah took her hand and turned down the street away from the hotel. Once more Ilsa felt that sense of utter rightness she'd experienced last night. Then he stopped, turning to face her, expression serious and eyes intense. 'I needed to make sure you hadn't changed your mind.' His fingers threaded through hers. 'Are you coming to Istanbul, Ilsa?'

She loved the way he said her name in a velvety rumble that made her twitch with pleasure. More, she loved

feeling that he too shared the heady excitement of this moment. That it was profound in some way.

Ilsa stood taller. She'd had time for doubts, but none had outweighed her need for what Noah offered. Escape. Adventure. Sexual pleasure. The chance simply to be herself, not burdened by public perception or royal rules.

'I am.'

For a second longer he looked grave, then his shoulders dropped as he exhaled and she wondered if he'd been holding his breath. A smile uncurled from the corner of his mouth and the sun shone brighter.

'I want to kiss you senseless,' he growled, 'but maybe that's not a good idea. Come on.' He started walking, still holding her hand.

'Where are we going?'

She sounded breathless but with good reason. The thought of Noah kissing her senseless...

'A little place I discovered that I hope you'll like.'

Noah's little place turned out to be just that. Tucked away in a back street, it had a tiny back terrace with a glimpse of the sea and a profusion of pot plants. It was busy but not with tourists or fashionable celebrities. It had the charm and bustle of an unpretentious eatery popular with locals.

'I didn't realise there were places like this still in the city. So down-to-earth,' she said as a waiter left a basket of crusty bread and a bowl of olives.

'You like it? I thought it best to have relative privacy. Give the gossips less to chew on.'

Ilsa nodded and reached for an olive. 'Good idea.

And I do like it. The scents are making my mouth water.'

'I'm glad.' His voice dropped to a low, intimate note. 'I want to please you.'

'Because you want me.'

Saying it aloud made Ilsa feel…powerful.

His lazy smile became a hungry grin that made her sit straighter, nipples peaking. 'I do. But there's pleasure to be had in simply seeing you happy.'

In another man she'd label that practised charm, but with Noah it felt real. Another first.

'You really are unique. I've met lots of men but none like you.' Noah lifted his eyebrows. 'You know what you want but you're not selfish about it.'

Last night she'd tried to mask the severity of her cramps, yet Noah had wanted to wake the onboard medic to check her. When she'd refused he'd insisted on sitting with her till the pain lessened before escorting her to her hotel. Ilsa couldn't recall anything like it, except once as a child when she was ill and her mother sat by her bed.

Then there was Noah's decision to visit Turkey because it was where *she* wanted to travel. Nor had he asked for details about the scandal of her recent past. That had earned her gratitude and respect.

She lusted after Noah Carson but *liked* him too. With him Ilsa felt she could unwind and be herself, whoever that was. She'd spent so long playing a role devised for her sometimes she wondered who the real Ilsa was.

'You've known a lot of selfish men?'

She thought of the man who'd professed to adore

her. Who'd wanted to make love to her. He'd moved to greener pastures when her mother took her away to the States. Her parents had been right. He'd played on her romantic dreams, hoping to carve a lucrative royal niche for himself at the expense of her heart. But he hadn't had the patience to wait for her.

'I've come across one or two.'

One or two dozen.

Noah's hand tightened around hers. 'If ever you want to talk, Ilsa...'

Her eyebrows shot up in surprise. A man wanting to talk? 'You really aren't what I expected.'

Did he stiffen? His eyes narrowed. 'What did you expect?'

She shrugged. 'After that charity lunch I did a quick internet search.' She'd stopped almost immediately when she saw the parade of lovely women through his life. 'The press paint you as brash, brilliant and with an eye for women.'

'Maybe I am.'

'Maybe.' She tilted her head, surveying him. 'I can see why you keep topping those Sexiest Men lists.' To her astonishment, his tanned cheeks darkened. 'Noah Carson, are you blushing?'

'As if.' He lifted his arm, fisting his hand and curling his biceps in parody of a bodybuilder while he waggled his eyebrows.

Ilsa smiled. He might be hamming it up, but the effect was real. He was strong, attractive and potently masculine. Something deep inside stirred into life and it wasn't another period cramp.

'You're probably brilliant, since I know you made your own fortune. But you're not brash.'

Again he shrugged. 'I've been told I'm rough around the edges.'

'Really?' She scanned his shoulders, his strong arms, then lifted her gaze back to his sculpted jaw and brilliant eyes. 'I like what I see.'

His grin melted her bones and she was glad she was sitting. 'Good.' He paused. 'But do you know my background?'

Ilsa shook her head. 'I already knew your name, and that you're Australian. But I didn't do a comprehensive search.'

She'd intended to last night. It made sense to know about him before she embarked on an affair. But despite her elation she'd been tired and sore and had slept instead.

'I wasn't born rich, so my background is different.'

Noah saw puzzlement in her blue-grey eyes.

He was intrigued by how they changed colour. Last night in that sexy dress they'd looked blue. But when he touched her and sometimes when he caught her looking at him, they blazed silver grey and mysterious. He wanted to explore all her mysteries, find out what turned her on and all her secrets.

It was a far cry from the casual feelings he usually had for lovers.

She's not your lover yet. Maybe she won't be, when she hears who you really are.

Was that why he'd engineered this discussion? To check she wasn't like Poppy?

But Poppy was eager to sleep with you. It was only when you naively wanted more—

'Everyone's background is different in some way,' said the woman born in line to take a throne. 'What?' She'd caught his rueful smile.

Noah shook his head. 'Some differences are more acceptable than others.'

There was no need to pursue this. But now he'd started, he wanted to see her reaction. He needed to be sure she wouldn't get cold feet after he left and change her mind about meeting him in Istanbul.

'Tell me about yours.'

He spread his shoulders in a shrug. 'My family is fantastic, warm and funny. Very encouraging and supportive. I grew up happy.' Long summer holidays playing cricket or going to the beach, until he was old enough to get a job and he'd started saving and planning.

'You're lucky.'

Ilsa smiled yet her tone made him wonder what it had been like growing up royal. Whatever she'd been through, he guessed it had taken a toll, though she was adept at hiding it.

'I know I'm lucky. When you asked last night what I wanted out of life I realised I already have it. A happy life with my family around me.' He was the first in his family to hit his thirties and not marry but his experience with Poppy had soured him on the idea. 'I don't want a wife and kids. Or even a long-term lover.' He caught Ilsa's gaze, making sure she understood the lim-

its to what he offered. 'I've got a large extended family and that's enough.'

'I understand.' Ilsa's tone was grave. 'You're not looking to start a family, just have some fun.' Yet something about her tone scraped his nerves, a note he couldn't identify. Then she continued. 'So, how was your family different?'

'My father and grandfather were garbos.' He saw her confusion and continued. 'That's Australian for garbage collectors. The ones who ride the trucks and empty the bins. Though now, with mechanised lifts on the trucks, those jobs are largely gone and it's mainly just driving.'

'And?'

'And what?'

She tilted her head as if to view him better. 'From your tone I'm waiting for something negative. Crime maybe. Violence?'

Was she serious? 'The Carsons are law-abiding. Hardworking but not in jobs people aspire to. Members of my family don't usually go to university.' He'd thought of it but he'd been too busy working. Once his business had begun expanding and diversifying it had seemed irrelevant.

Still Ilsa only nodded.

'Do you know where I started my business? Not trading shares or buying real estate, but with a clapped-out old truck, contracted to do a rural garbage run. Then another, and another. Clearly your online research wasn't thorough. From time to time the press call me *The King of Trash.*'

Imagine the furore if, instead of sharing a short af-

fair with Ilsa, a man like him wanted something more permanent. All hell would break out, including in her oh-so-royal family. Just as well he wasn't in the market for long-term.

'I read that you'd invested in making road surfaces and other things from old tyres. So you run a waste management business?'

Far from being deterred, Ilsa looked interested. It wasn't what he'd expected.

'Partly, but it's extended far beyond that. It began with collection and disposal but our main focus is reuse and recycling. We've invested in a range of innovations that have done well and there are opportunities everywhere.'

Many projects were on an industrial scale, using the expertise of scientists and engineers, while others were grass roots schemes, some in developing countries. The latter mightn't make big profits but it was amazing how innovations in one area leapfrogged from an initiative somewhere else.

'And this is what makes you *rough around the edges*?'

Noah paused as the waiter served their meals but he didn't make a move to eat. 'Dealing with waste isn't what most people aspire to.'

It certainly wasn't a family business Poppy had wanted to marry into. To her he'd been good enough for sex. He'd been an up-and-coming entrepreneur, different to the men her family approved, who had old money and old school ties helping them up the greasy pole. But when Noah naively believed himself in love

and asked her to marry him she'd been aghast. As if a whiff of the garbage heap would mar the nuptials. Not that it had stopped her trying to get money from him to support her start-up business.

Then there was the damage she'd done to his sister.

Ally had been in her teens and slavishly devoted to Poppy, who'd enjoyed her adulation. Ally was the one person in his family Poppy had time for, even inviting her to some events with her fashionable friends.

It was only later, as Ally battled depression and bulimia, that he'd learned how negatively Poppy and her friends had impacted his sister. They were so obsessed with appearances. All those comments about her needing to lose weight and the importance of looking model-thin at all costs had taken their toll. Poppy had dumped his sister cruelly too when she'd rejected Noah, leaving Ally battling the belief she wasn't good enough to be her friend.

Ilsa's sharp retort cut across his thoughts. 'You don't need me to tell you to ignore people who put you down because your family earned honest wages doing hard work.' She paused, her eyes flashing bright blue. 'Or did you expect *me* to think less of you for that?'

It was the first time Noah had seen her angry and he was torn between wanting to placate her and admiring how alluring she looked, her cheeks tinted with warmth and eyes sparkling. His skin tightened in response, as if showered by incendiary sparks.

'Not necessarily.'

He reached out and covered her hand where it rested

on the table. A second later she withdrew it, cradling her fingers in her lap. It was a first and he didn't like it.

Her face told him nothing. It was composed and un-readable, except for those brilliant eyes.

'I didn't know,' he finally admitted. 'It matters to some people.'

Not anyone whose opinion was important to him.

Ilsa's opinion mattered, though. It surprised him how much.

'Your work is important. Managing our resources better is vital. As for looking down on you because of the family business…'

'What?' he asked finally when she let the words hang.

'Aren't you guilty of the same? Did you think I'd wrinkle my nose because of what *my* family does? Because I was born royal?'

Noah stared. That was precisely what he'd done, even if with some reason, given his history with Poppy. 'You're right. I did.'

He should have known better.

Still she sat unbending, chin up and shoulders back. Even in a simple summer dress of misty blue and no jewellery other than discreet gold earrings, she looked regal. He wanted her so badly. He couldn't bear the idea of her pulling away from him now.

'Being royal isn't about wearing ermine and going to balls. My great-grandfather's proudest achievement was having a modern network of sewers built under the capital. And if you talk to my father he'd tell you that managing waste collection in a severe alpine win-

ter is an ongoing challenge. Two of his major priorities are making our nation self-sustainable and reducing its waste footprint.'

'Touché.' Noah laughed, raising his hands in a gesture of surrender. 'I stand corrected.'

'I'm *not* my status, Noah. I might have an aristocratic title but that's not all I am.'

His laughter died. He'd struck a nerve. For the first time since they'd met she looked haughty. Not because he'd forgotten she was a princess, but because he'd remembered!

Noah leaned closer. Was that hurt in her eyes?

'I apologise, Ilsa.' He drew a slow breath. 'Having been the subject of prejudice myself I should have known better.'

He took a sip of water to remove the sour taste in his mouth, then laid his arm across the table, palm up, inviting her touch.

'When I'm with you I don't think of you as Your Royal Highness.' Not since they'd met on the dance floor last night. Noah's voice dropped to a gravel note. 'You're too down-to-earth, too sexy, generous and too much fun to fit my idea of royalty. You fascinate me.'

Her hand, smaller and softer than his, touched his palm. Instantly he folded his fingers around hers, feeling his blood pump faster at the connection.

'I want you for the woman you are behind the title, Ilsa.'

Emotion flared in her eyes and the pulse at her wrist beat hectically. Then the tip of her tongue swiped her pink lips and he almost groaned aloud. She seduced

him as no woman ever had. The idea of waiting another week…

'That's the nicest thing anyone's ever said to me.'

She leaned across and brushed her lips across his
cheek in a feather-light caress that jolted a few thousand volts through him.

Want. It was an insipid word. He'd known her such
a short time and every moment had been torture and
delight. Delight because she was everything and more
than he'd dared hope and torture because sexual frustration reached its limit.

He didn't merely want Ilsa. He *craved* her.

No woman had affected him the way Princess Ilsa
of Altbourg did, or so instantaneously.

His breath rasped in his throat and he jerked back
in his chair.

'What's wrong, Noah?'

He made himself release her hand, pretending an
interest in his meal. 'Nothing's wrong. But we need to
eat before I do something that will totally scandalise
the other diners.'

Later that week, Ilsa returned to her hotel from the
royal dinner, resplendent in satin and jewels. It had been
lovely, more enjoyable than she'd expected, but as she
entered her room and stepped out of her high heels her
overriding emotion was relief that finally she was free
of royal commitments. Soon she'd fly to Istanbul to
meet Noah.

Her phone rang and her heart leapt. Noah! She
snatched it up.

'Ilsa.'

Her pounding heart stopped for a moment then sank. 'Father.'

Half an hour later she ended the call and stared, unseeing, at the landscape painting on the wall, her brain whirling. The King had supposedly rung to discuss that evening's function and various diplomatic matters that had been raised with her hosts.

There had been more too but, to her surprise, not condemnation about her being seen leaving the yacht club with Noah Carson. For once her father had held back, not lecturing about what she owed her royal dignity.

That had thrown her.

He'd flummoxed her further by saying he understood the last months had been tough, hinting at sympathy that her direction in life was no longer simple. Of course he never referred to the fact she'd spent years training to rule Altbourg but was now no longer his heir. Instead he'd reflected that she was old enough to know what she was doing, only adding that he hoped she didn't do anything she'd regret.

He'd ended by mentioning a recent deal Noah had done with a French consortium, saying he'd like to interest Noah in a similar project for Altbourg. Would she raise that with Noah? Persuade him to visit and discuss a proposal?

Slightly dazed at not being read the riot act by her father, Ilsa had agreed.

She frowned and rubbed her forehead with her fingertips. Could it be that he was finally treating her as an independent adult rather than a royal pawn? As for

asking Noah to consider a business opportunity in her homeland, why not? If that was the price of keeping her father sweet she'd happily do it.

Ilsa rolled her shoulders and sank back in her chair, revelling in the sudden feeling of utter freedom. It was wonderful but daunting at the same time.

She no longer had a clear role mapped out for her, either as ruler of her own country or as consort to a royal husband in Vallort.

She'd have to decide what she wanted to do, carve out a role that satisfied her duty to and love of her country, but pleased her too.

That was for the long term. For now, all she could focus on was seeing Noah again, pursuing the attraction between them and embarking on her first ever love affair.

CHAPTER FIVE

ILSA WAS MET at the airport by a stranger who escorted her to a limousine. He was friendly but it was an effort to respond to his conversation. She'd expected Noah.

Nerves hit and her stomach churned. Had she been right to come?

Maybe he'd changed his mind. Maybe he regretted his invitation.

But Noah would have told her.

Her bemusement grew as they drove away from the city, until the driver explained that she was to join the yacht. When they reached the sea it was almost dark. But there was a speedboat waiting for her and out on the darkening water a familiar graceful yacht.

Ilsa's heart leapt even as her palms grew clammy, doubts surfacing.

But when she finally climbed aboard there was Noah, reaching for her, pulling her close so she felt his heat envelop her. His eyes were so bright and hungry that exultation rushed through her.

'Ilsa, at last.' His fingers meshed with hers. 'I wanted to come to the airport but I didn't want to draw atten-

tion to the fact we were together. I thought you'd prefer to keep that quiet as long as possible.'

That banished her flurry of nerves and she smiled. 'Thank you. I hadn't even thought of that.'

Her mind had been fogged thinking about him.

'Come inside.' He led her through into a familiar lounge. 'If you're not tired I thought we could have a drink and watch as we approach the city. It's supposed to be spectacular.'

'I'd like that.'

'Good.' He squeezed her hand then headed to the bar, leaving Ilsa disappointed that he hadn't kissed her hello. She'd dreamed of his kisses and so much more.

'Here you are.'

Noah handed her a tall glass and she laughed. 'Cherry juice!'

'Freshly made. The galley is well stocked with fresh fruit for you.'

She tilted her head to one side, surveying him. He was as vital and gorgeous as she recalled and she found it hard to catch her breath when he was close. But it was the laughter in his eyes and his obvious pleasure at her delight that made her pulse quicken.

'That's very considerate. Thank you.'

'Don't look so surprised.'

She shrugged. 'Maybe I'm more used to people focused on what *they* want.'

He put down his glass and took her hand. 'Believe me, Ilsa, I'm *very* focused on what I want.' His voice dropped to an abrasive note that drew her skin tight in delicious anticipation.

'Yet you haven't even kissed me.'

Ilsa caught her breath. She hadn't planned to say it but the words spilled out. Because she was frustrated by the distance he maintained while she hungered for more.

She could have initiated a kiss, but something prevented her. Lack of expertise. Or a shadow of doubt? The only other man who'd professed to want her had lied. He'd been more concerned with her status than her.

Noah squeezed her fingers then let go, shoving his hands into his pockets, leaving her dismayed.

'Noah?'

Why the withdrawal? He'd looked at her as if he wanted to eat her up and his words had implied just that. But she didn't have the experience or the confidence to be sure.

'What do you want me to say, Ilsa?'

His gaze dropped to her mouth and she felt it like a graze, her lips tingling in response. Heat shuddered through her, that strange hollow feeling low in her body teasing her again.

'The truth. Only ever the truth.' She'd had enough of prevarication and polite lies to last a lifetime.

'You know the truth.' His voice hummed low and soft, the sound of pure seduction. 'I want you. Badly. Of course I want to kiss you. All over.' He watched her eyes widen and his mouth snagged up at one side in a smile that looked like a grimace. 'I want to feast on you slowly, Ilsa. And then I want to...'

He closed his eyes and shook his head. She fought the urge to plant her mouth on his. To grab his shoulders and press herself against him from head to toe.

His eyes snapped open and she saw raw longing

there. She recognised it because she saw it daily in the mirror.

Noah swallowed, the movement jerky. Finally she noticed the rigid set of his shoulders and the tight clench of his jaw. She'd been so wrapped up in her response to his words she hadn't read the signs.

'I haven't kissed you because when we do there'll be no stopping. But I need to wait till you're ready.' His voice was rough, almost brutal. Yet Ilsa had never heard anything more wonderful. 'Unless you want to be ravished on the spot, kissing will need to wait until you're ready for more.'

Her chest rose shakily as relief flooded. He'd promised her time. Yet self-doubt and unrequited longing had made her wonder. It still seemed incredible that this stunning man should desire her, a woman no man had ever hungered for before.

'You're right. That will have to wait a little longer. But—' she paused '—I'm looking forward to it.'

Noah's breath hissed and she imagined him scooping her up and stalking off with her, because his patience had reached its limit. Excitement raced through her.

'So am I, Ilsa. You have no idea how much.'

By mutual consent they moved apart, not wanting to test their willpower. Even so the rest of that evening became etched in her memory as one of the best of her life.

The ancient city glittered like a thousand jewels displayed just for them under a black velvet sky. The dark water shimmered with lights from ashore and from other boats.

She and Noah stood on deck as they sailed in. Ilsa

caught her breath at the floodlit dome and delicate minarets of the Blue Mosque. Then there was the ancient dome of Hagia Sophia and the clustering compound of buildings that was Topkapi Palace, where generations of Sultans had lived. They passed the Golden Horn and the grand Dolmabahçe Palace spreading along the waterfront. Ilsa was glad her first sight of the city was at night, when its beauty seemed more fairy tale than real.

Finally Noah took her ashore to a magnificent, traditional mansion right on the water. Several storeys high, it had tall windows and beautiful ornamentation, as lovely as anything she'd seen in Venice. The ceilings soared and the spacious rooms were decorated in an elegant style that bordered on the romantic.

He'd rented the house rather than book into a hotel or travel to and from the yacht. Because this would give them privacy.

Ilsa's heart softened again at Noah's thoughtfulness. He made her feel that she truly mattered to him.

It was the most wonderful gift she'd ever received.

That night, as she lay in her vast bed, watching the lights reflected on the dark water, she decided Noah was unlike any man she'd known. He heated her blood with a smile. Made her heart turn over with his thoughtfulness. The more time she spent with him, the more she wanted.

She just hoped she didn't come to want too much.

This could only ever be a holiday fling.

Exploring the city with Ilsa was eye-opening.

She was carefree and alluring. Everywhere she drew

attention with her smile. She'd looked a million dollars wearing sequins and come-take-me heels, but casually dressed, her hair in a ponytail, she bowled Noah over. Again.

A discreet security team guaranteed they weren't bothered by paparazzi but didn't interfere as Ilsa smiled and chatted her way through the streets.

She talked to fishermen, leaning out from a bridge with their rods. She paused to admire water-sellers in bright clothes, carrying ornate metal urns on their backs, and others selling snacks like peeled cucumbers dipped in salt or rounds of sesame bread.

People were eager to talk with her. She exuded a warmth that drew them like moths to candlelight.

He'd thought from some things she said that public events were a chore. Now he mused that it wasn't the public she disliked, but something else. Something to do with royal protocols and arrangements, perhaps.

Suddenly he found himself curious again about her failed engagements.

He longed to know more but refused to probe.

Noah had wondered too what she'd want to see in the city. The fabled treasury of the sultans? Instead she'd suggested the covered market. Shopping, of course, he should have guessed. Except, instead of going to the Grand Bazaar, Ilsa opted for the Spice Market.

Just inside the door Ilsa's hand slipped into his. 'Isn't it amazing?'

'It is.' The scents hit him. A thousand flavours mingling and filling the air. Beneath the high, arched roof was a kaleidoscope of colours.

Already Ilsa was browsing a shop display. Cones of brightly coloured spices. Open sacks revealing blends of teas, peppercorns, whole spices and nuts.

'What are you shopping for?'

'I'm just exploring. Though that tea with the dried rosebuds looks intriguing. I know someone who'd love that.'

They investigated every part of the market. Noah wasn't renowned for his patience with shopping, but this was different.

Watching Ilsa's face light on discovering some new delicacy was a treat. Hearing her banter with stallholders, basking in her vibrant warmth as she turned to include him in the conversation was actually…fun.

She had asked him what made him happy and he'd instantly thought of his family. Now, remarkably, Noah realised being with Ilsa came close.

They hadn't even slept together. He was in permanent discomfort, on the edge of arousal. He should be climbing the walls with frustration and resentment, and it was true his nights were a torture of unfulfilled erotic dreams. Surely tomorrow…

'Are you okay, Noah?' She turned to him with a big package of Turkish delight in her hands.

He took the package and tucked it under his arm. 'Why wouldn't I be?'

She frowned at the package as if about to insist she carry it, then shrugged. 'Because I've kept you here. Are you bored?'

'Surprisingly, no. It's been a revelation.'

Shimmering blue-grey eyes considered him as she smiled. 'It's marvellous, isn't it?'

'Absolutely.' Noah wasn't thinking of the market but her. He slid his hand beneath her elbow. Because he couldn't *not* touch her. 'When are you going to eat all these sweets?'

He'd seen her delight at breakfast when she'd found rose petal jelly and a pitcher of fresh cherry juice along with bread and an array of savoury foods. But, despite her sweet tooth, Ilsa didn't have the body of a woman who overindulged.

She had a slender waist and long, lithe legs, her curves just the right size to tantalise...

'It's not for me. There are people in Altbourg who'll love them.' She paused. 'Now, where would you like to go?'

Noah shook his head. 'It's your first visit. You choose.'

'Really?' She hesitated. 'There's something else I've heard about that I'd like to buy, if you'll brave the Grand Bazaar.'

'As long as you appreciate what a sacrifice more shopping will be.'

She leaned close, her breast pressing his arm and shooting fire to his groin. Her light scent of bergamot and warm feminine skin hit his sense receptors like a promise of endless pleasure. 'I promise to reward you.'

Noah firmed his grip on her arm, wanting so much more.

'I'll hold you to that,' he growled.

She blinked, eyes widening. Was that excitement he

saw, or nerves? No, Ilsa wasn't nervous. Her body told its own tale of thwarted longing.

'I'll look forward to it. Meanwhile, lunch is on me.'

Instead of a posh restaurant, they grazed on delicious street food, Ilsa ordering enough for the security professionals he'd thought she hadn't even noticed. But then she'd have had such teams around her from birth. Her world was so different, even with his success and fortune as equalisers.

Their visit to the Grand Bazaar passed quickly, though it was an endless Aladdin's cave. It was crammed with shops boasting everything from leather goods to ceramics, metalwork, carpets, lamps and ornaments.

Soon they were seated, drinking apple tea while Ilsa inspected quaint leather slippers topped with brightly striped satin. Their upturned toes made them look like something from an *Arabian Nights* illustration.

Noah was distracted by a woman two shops away who raised her phone in their direction. He couldn't protect Ilsa from every photographer, though he'd like to. Already there'd been plenty of speculation about them.

'Perfect. I'll take four dozen in the full range of children's sizes.'

'Four dozen?' He swung his head around and leaned closer. 'Plans for a big family?' he murmured.

Ilsa stiffened. Then he decided he'd imagined it as she rolled her eyes at him before giving the vendor a shipping address. The children's ward in an Altbourg hospital.

Noah sat back.

She spent her holiday buying gifts for sick kids.

It was a thoughtful, personal gesture. Ilsa could have asked a staff member to organise presents but she'd done it herself. It wasn't just the buying, it was thinking about those children during a time that was supposed to be just for her.

Noah's chest constricted as if a balloon inflated behind his ribs. It took a moment to recognise the sensation. Pride. For a woman who really cared.

Five minutes later they were outside. Noah braced himself for more shopping. But Ilsa insisted he choose their next destination.

The Yerabatan Cistern was an ancient underground reservoir held up by hundreds of towering marble columns. They strolled in the half-darkness on raised walkways, strategic lighting turning the shallow water below them to shot silk. It was amazing and atmospheric.

'How did you know about this place?' Ilsa murmured, shifting closer as they surveyed an enormous stone Medusa head at the base of a column. The fact that the monumental head, with carved snakes in its hair, was upside down, made the blank eyes strangely disturbing.

Noah gave up resisting temptation. He roped his arm around Ilsa, his hand on her cool arm. Immediately two things happened. His hold tightened instinctively and she leaned in, making his heart thud.

He wanted to wrap both arms around her, pull her between his legs and ease the ache in his groin. He wanted to set his mouth on hers, as he'd been desperate to do from the moment he'd seen her sitting, prim and ridiculously seductive, at that charity lunch.

She turned, her chin lifting, and he sucked in air, ready to kiss her.

'Noah? How did you discover this? It's amazing.'

He fought the urge to kiss her till her blood caught fire like his. Except, once stoked, there'd be only one way to quench that fire. Besides, the gloom might screen other visitors, but didn't guarantee privacy.

Noah usually ignored the press but he knew a public airing of Ilsa's personal life had hurt her before. The press was already breathless with speculation about them. He wouldn't draw further attention.

Noah drew a tight breath and fought for control. 'Would you believe I saw this place in a film?'

Her lips curved up and it hit him, again, that she had a sweet smile. As well as a full, passionate mouth. He wanted those lips on him, all over him. He wanted—

'I can believe it. What a great setting.'

A flash exploded from behind a nearby column. It was probably some amateur photographer trying to catch the grandeur of the place. But it was a timely reminder.

Noah stepped away, ignoring an internal roar of protest.

'It's time we left.' This had to stop. He made a show of looking at his watch. 'I have a video conference.'

One he'd only just decided to accept, to put some distance between them.

Yet, even as he decided to accept the invitation, it felt like a mistake. Not because it was bad business; it sounded like an exciting opportunity. But because he'd rather spend the rest of the day with Ilsa.

'Oh. Of course.'

Was that disappointment? Ilsa's expression gave nothing away. Perversely, that annoyed him.

'Perhaps I'll come too.'

Perhaps? Why had he supposed she'd return with him? It stunned Noah how uncomfortable he felt at the idea of her wandering the city without him. The security staff would protect her but he wanted her near him, even as he tried to stay sane by putting space between them.

What did that say about his state of mind? He wasn't accustomed to such possessiveness.

Noah ran his hand through his hair, ignoring the sudden prickle of dampness at his hairline. It was just sexual frustration, magnifying desire so it felt like something else.

Ilsa put her hand on his arm. 'Since you mention business, there was something I forgot to ask. Might you be interested in a project in Altbourg? My father heard about a project you're planning in France and is very enthusiastic...'

Three hours later he ended the video call and leaned back in the desk chair.

His mouth ticked up at the corner. He might have agreed to the discussion to get some space from temptation, but it had been a good business decision. He shot off a message to his team, arranging follow-up.

Someone knocked. Probably the housekeeper, seeing if he needed refreshments.

'Come.'

The ornate door swung open and Ilsa stepped in.

Noah's gut contracted. His breath, when he finally managed to release it, sighed out between his teeth.

Her hair spilled around her shoulders, golden as a summer sunrise. Her dress, azure blue and lustrous, was moulded to her upper body before flaring out to end high above her knees. Which left those long, slender legs bare.

His gaze tracked down to spindle-heeled sandals that consisted of miniscule straps the same colour as her dress.

He raised his eyes, pausing of necessity at her breasts, their sweet upper swell just revealed by the straight edge of the fabric.

The dress was held up by straps so thin they looked as if they'd tear with one tug of a finger, or his teeth.

'Ilsa.' Her name was gruff in his mouth. He swallowed. He needed to sound amiable, not like a man wanting to eat her up centimetre by slow centimetre. 'You look rested.'

She looked bloody fabulous.

Desirable yet understated.

Except for the sandals. They screamed sex so loud it interfered with his hearing.

'Sorry?' He'd seen her lips move but hadn't heard the words.

'I asked if you'd finished your business.'

'Yes.'

He'd planned to stay here, sending a few emails before torturing himself with her company over dinner. But, faced with the sight of her in the flesh, the silky, alluring flesh, all thought of contracts and due diligence disintegrated.

Ilsa took another step and pushed the door shut behind her. She paused and he saw her breasts push up against the constraint of the shimmery dress.

His mouth dried again. If he tried to talk he'd sound like a bear woken from hibernation. Or a man losing control of his libido.

She turned the key in the lock.

Noah's heart hammered against his ribs, sending every blood cell to his groin as excitement rose.

'Why are you here, Ilsa?' His voice was so rough he wondered if she'd understand the words.

'I want to kiss you, Noah.' His heart stopped then stuttered back to life. 'I want…everything.'

CHAPTER SIX

ILSA'S HEART DID a crazy slalom in her chest and her knees locked, making her stop, her hand on the door.

She'd deliberately not worn a bra and as she drew a deep breath the graze of fabric against her nipples was disconcerting. And arousing.

Noah stood behind a massive desk, looking potently masculine. Worn jeans clung to powerful thighs and his pale shirt emphasised both the breadth of his straight shoulders and the colour of those remarkable turquoise eyes below straight black brows.

She loved that intense hooded stare of his, the way it made her feel utterly feminine and alluring.

Yet this time she also felt a flutter of anxiety.

Her hand tightened on the key.

It was ridiculous to be nervous. Except this was new territory. Her one previous foray into romance hadn't been consummated.

Yet surely this was the most natural thing in the world. A man and woman drawn to each other.

She'd wanted Noah from the moment she'd seen him.

Her desire had only strengthened as she got to know

him. There was so much to admire. He kept his word, he cared about others, not just himself. He noticed, listened, encouraged. He was fun and charming and...

He had the most fantastic body. Those hard, shifting muscles, powerful limbs and taut backside. The determined chin. That mobile, laughing mouth that promised all sorts of delight.

She wanted to rip his clothes off and quench the empty ache deep inside.

'You're ready?'

Noah's voice was hot treacle over gravel, making her shudder and sending a spike of sensation straight to the apex of her thighs. She shifted her weight, feeling telltale moisture as her body softened there.

Yet he didn't move. Instead his broad brow knotted.

Was it possible he'd changed his mind? Ilsa had spent ages bathing and primping. Had she got it wrong?

Suddenly she felt overdressed in silk and heels. She'd scoured her wardrobe for something sexy. This dress, like the sequinned one, had been an impulse buy in Monaco. She'd thought both said fun and carefree. But maybe it was too plain. She wished she owned a black lace negligee.

'I'm ready.' She lifted her chin. 'If you are, Noah.' She stepped forward then stopped, amazed to find her knees wobbling.

Suddenly Noah was there, right before her.

His hands circled her upper arms supportively. 'Are you okay?'

Ilsa read concern in his voice. Yet he looked at her with hot eyes that made her think of summer seas and

searing sex. He *hadn't* changed his mind. He'd simply responded to her tension.

A slow smile curved her lips and she watched his gaze drop to her mouth. 'I've never felt better.'

Ilsa was surprised that her legs could feel weak when the rest of her coursed with energy as if she'd been zapped by an electric current. She swallowed and circled her dry mouth with the tip of her tongue.

Something flickered in Noah's eyes that made her heart leap. He released her arms and instead wrapped his arms around her, pulling her hard against him.

Yes! Glorious sensations bombarded her from breast to knee. She slid her arms over his shoulders, tilting her head to his as she strained closer.

His lips, she discovered, were cool and surprisingly soft, covering her mouth lightly in a caress that didn't feel tentative but tender.

The impression lasted just long enough for her to identify it. Then one large hand rose to the back of her skull, holding her as Noah angled his head for better access and plunged deep into her mouth.

Ilsa gasped and held on tight as gentle and questing became demanding. Her breasts peaked and fire roared in her veins as she pressed against him and devoured him right back.

She hadn't kissed since her teens and eagerness made her clumsy. Plus the fact that the kisses in her past hadn't prepared her for Noah's unbridled passion. The passion they shared. She was on fire and the only way to put it out was incinerating herself in the conflagration he'd ignited inside her.

Ilsa's nose bumped Noah's and she grazed his tongue with her teeth. But, instead of pulling back, he shuddered, his hold tightening as a low growl emanated from his throat.

He liked it. And the sound of his approval ratcheted up her own urgency.

She slid her tongue against his, bolder now, giving herself up to the magic they made. When she used her teeth again he planted both hands on her and lifted her up so she felt his erection right where she needed him.

Ilsa tilted her hips, desperate for more. Hunger was a consuming force, taking over her whole body.

Her fingers speared his soft hair as their kiss accelerated into blazing intensity. Her chest heaved, her heart hammering, but she needed his mouth on hers. She couldn't break away, even to breathe.

Until Noah pulled his head back, surveying her through narrowed, glittering eyes.

The air was thick with the sound of laboured breathing, charged as if from a sparking live wire.

Ilsa slid her hands around to cup his jawline, fingers splaying possessively over taut skin and hard bone, her thumb swiping his reddened bottom lip. She wanted to touch him all over with her hands and her mouth, discover the grain and texture and taste of him.

Noah's lips parted just enough that he could suck her thumb into his mouth, drawing against it as his gaze pinioned hers. She arched, pressing her pelvis and her breasts against him. He sucked hard at her thumb and she shuddered helplessly as traceries of fire ignited in

her blood, from her nipples to her womb. Between her legs she felt lush dampness.

Ilsa opened her mouth to say something, she wasn't sure what, when the room wheeled.

Noah shifted his grip, lifting her off her feet and swinging her round. Then she was sitting on the desk, Noah standing between her legs, pushing them wide.

It felt deliciously decadent but it still wasn't enough.

He used his teeth on her thumb, just a tiny nip, but it made her shudder, squirming further forward on the desktop, pressing herself against the bulge in his jeans.

In response he pressed his palm against her lower back, holding her close while his other hand shaped her braless breast through the fabric. Ilsa's eyelids lowered as she pushed into his big hand, her body tightening in delight at the unfamiliar sensation. Had anything ever felt so delicious?

He pressed kisses along her thumb then her palm. 'I'd imagined our first time in a bed with a full box of condoms. But this works.' He moved his hips and the friction of denim on silk made her eyes roll back.

Condoms! Her brain snapped into gear.

How could she not have thought of that? She'd been so busy dressing to seduce and imagining the bliss of Noah's naked body, she'd forgotten the basics. Locking the study door had been an impulse. She'd fully expected them to end up in Noah's bed.

She blinked up at him. 'I'm sorry. I don't have one.' Some seductress she was.

Noah grinned, reaching into his back pocket and drawing out a couple of square packets.

'Ever since you came to Istanbul I've carried protection, just in case.' The look he gave her melted a vital organ or two. 'Now, where were we up to?'

He reached around her and found her zip, lowering it slowly, the slide of his fingers against her flesh incredibly arousing. As was the look in his eyes.

'I like that you don't wear a bra with this.'

He spread his hand across her bare back and lowered his head. Ilsa raised her mouth to his but instead Noah kissed her neck, finding a spot near the curve to her shoulder that made her writhe and grab at him. His mouth skated past her collarbone to the tiny spaghetti strap. A second later he closed his teeth around it and dragged it off her shoulder, making the bodice droop on that side, almost revealing her breast.

Ilsa shifted, her thigh muscles clenching as his knowing gaze met hers. Did he realise she was wet between the legs for him?

He dipped his head and dragged the other strap down too.

'Take your arms out of the dress, Ilsa.'

It was an order, his tone brusque. But, instead of being annoyed, she was excited because she read urgency in his glazed eyes and hard body.

She shrugged the rest of the way free of the straps and heard his breath hiss. For a long moment he didn't touch her, just looked, and she forgot that this was her first time and she needed to warn him, lest he be disappointed. She was too caught up in feeling sexy and wanted.

Gently he lowered her to the desktop, pushing away

something that thudded to the floor, then put his mouth on her breast.

Nothing had prepared her for the riot of sensation. For such sharp desire. His mouth, and his hand on her other breast, fogged her brain and turned her into a keening, desperate woman. She heard the wild gasps, knew they came from her mouth, but couldn't stop them.

She held him to her breast with hands that shook. But it wasn't enough. She needed more.

Wriggling for purchase, she lifted one leg around his solid thigh, then the other, trying to get closer to all that lovely heat.

Brilliant eyes met hers as he licked her nipple then lifted his head.

'I like your thinking,' he growled, scrabbling at her skirt.

Finally she felt him, flesh to flesh, his hand between her legs.

Noah's eyes rounded as he realised she wore no underwear. 'I *do* like your thinking! If I'd known from the start you had nothing on under this dress…'

He shook his head as his fingers slid and explored.

Ilsa couldn't stay still. With every caress she *had* to move. Every touch sent her closer and closer to the edge.

Lifting her hips, she arched high, her eyes closing as tremulous shivers of anticipation started inside.

When Noah took his hand away she frowned and snapped her eyes open, in time to see him tug at his own zip as he tore the condom packet with his teeth.

Ilsa had expected this moment would seem weighty and significant. She'd thought of telling him she was a virgin. But all that mattered was their need for each other.

Excitement and desire melded with something that made her chest feel full as she watched Noah frown in concentration.

She'd heard enough to expect her first time mightn't be perfect but didn't care. Next time would be better. Already he'd made her feel so very, very good. Not just aroused, but admired and appreciated. *Special*.

She wanted Noah with every cell in her yearning body. She refused to break this precious moment with a confession, as if lack of experience needed an apology.

So when he leaned over her, his chest bare now, his breath hot on her face and his shoulders blocking the room, she simply reached up and pulled him close. The weight of his erection teased her slick flesh. She knew a moment's surprise at how large he felt, but it was nothing to the compulsion to give herself and have him finally satisfy her craving.

'Ilsa.' She drowned in those tropical eyes. 'I want you so much I can't promise to last long.'

Then, before she could think of a response, Noah pushed slow and deep.

Ilsa's breath caught. She felt her eyes widen at the unfamiliar sensation, heavy, full and disorientating. She gasped as he paused when discomfort dragged at her. Then, after a second, Noah hitched her leg higher, up around his waist, and everything felt easier. With his help she wrapped her other leg higher, clinging to him as the almost-pain ebbed.

Even then he didn't move. Just leaned above her, chest heaving.

Ilsa slid her hands restlessly across his shoulders,

feeling the damp heat of his silky flesh. She shifted, clenching her muscles, and felt him shudder.

He was close to the brink, shaking, she realised, with the effort of not moving. Because he'd read her body's instinctive shock. But the shock was gone, replaced by a need to move and even more, have Noah lose himself with her.

Tentatively she circled her hips and was rewarded with a smooth thrust that took him deep to her core. So deep it felt as if she'd discovered life's greatest mystery.

Or maybe that was the effect of his silent gaze, locked on hers as if there was nothing in the world but them, together.

Holding on tight, wanting, above everything, to give Noah pleasure, she squeezed every muscle and felt him shudder. He withdrew and thrust again, faster, breath ragged and eyes glazing.

Triumph filled her and something softer, delight at his pleasure.

Abruptly everything changed. Noah leaned closer, his broad chest against her breasts, the friction of his body hair teasing her to full arousal again. Or maybe it was the way he nipped at her earlobe as his hand slid to that nub between her legs where sensation centred.

'Come with me, Ilsa,' he breathed against her ear. 'Come fly with me.'

His voice grated deliciously as he took her again, his fingers pressing hard, his teeth grazing her neck until the climax came out of nowhere. It rushed in, shattering her senses, her body, her ability to do more than gasp and hold tight as Noah bucked one last time then shuddered, pulsing within her.

Her senses overloaded. Pleasure frayed her thoughts, taking her into infinite space where there was nothing but ecstasy, and this man, anchoring her to sanity.

Finally, as she came back to herself, she registered the addictive scent of him filling her nostrils. The taste of him on her tongue. The rasp of their gasping breaths. His weight, hot and heavy but oh-so-perfect, his chest palpitating from effort. The last pulses of his body as he shared his essence with her.

Emotion rose and filled every corner of her being. Elation. Gratitude. Satisfaction. Wonder. Greed. Tenderness.

And something else that she had no name for. Something profound. She knew if she could see herself in the mirror there'd be stars in her eyes. But what she felt in her heart...

No one had warned her that her first experience of sex would make her so emotional. That she'd want to stay in her lover's arms for ever. That for the first time she could remember everything would feel *right*.

Not simply because of the physical pleasure but because with Noah she felt...

Drowsily she opened her eyes and looked straight into his. Her heart leapt.

For a second fear tickled her nape. Not fear of Noah but of how she felt about him. How tremendous the emotions bubbling inside her, when she knew this could only be a short affair.

Then he smiled and she bundled her fear to the back of her mind and told herself everything would be okay.

CHAPTER SEVEN

NOAH TRACED HIS finger from Ilsa's bare shoulder, down her arm. The rest of her body was covered by the sheet she'd tucked beneath her arm.

Her tiny shiver of response was echoed by the look in her drowsy eyes.

Strange that such a sensuous woman, a woman who'd brazenly marched into his office wearing no underwear, should be so modest about covering her beautiful body.

But then she didn't make a habit of parading half-naked for other men. She'd been a virgin.

Questions crammed his brain. And regrets. He'd put her slightly clumsy kisses down to rampant enthusiasm, not inexperience. Should he have realised sooner?

Not when she'd pressed that hot body to his and purred her pleasure in his ear. The sounds she'd made when he took her breasts in his hands and mouth had driven him wild. And the feel of her reaching her pinnacle around him, the sight of her eyes blazing silver with ecstasy, had blasted the last of his control to smithereens.

'What are you thinking?' Noah looked up to find Ilsa's sleepy eyes on him. 'You look serious.'

'Just wondering if I should have taken more time and showed more finesse.'

Her mouth twitched at the corners and heat stirred in his groin. Again. He only had to look at her to want her.

'I thought you showed incredible finesse. We barely slopped any water out of the bath. Even though it's big enough for two we were both rather…enthusiastic.'

The twitch of her lips became a siren's smile and Noah let out a pent-up sigh. He'd spent the last half hour trying not to think about sex with Ilsa and failing miserably. It had been an eventful couple of hours and he should give her time to recuperate. He'd only joined her in the bed because she'd wrapped her arms around him and refused to let him go when he carried her from the bath.

'I was talking about the first time. In the study.'

'You didn't like doing it on the desk?' Her brow furrowed. 'I thought—' She bit off the words and her gaze slid away.

Noah reached out, cupping her cheek and turning her head so she met his eyes. 'Of course I liked it. I can't remember being so turned on in my life.'

'Really?' Her eyes sparkled.

She had no idea. 'You're a very sexy woman, Ilsa.' He remembered her challenging stare as she locked the door and the blast of shock when he discovered she was naked under that flimsy blue dress. His groin grew heavy and tight. 'I wanted you so much I was scared I'd come to grief just putting the condom on.'

Her mouth curved again in a smile that made him

think of a cat licking cream. She looked pleased, gloating even.

'I'm glad. I wasn't sure if you'd like it.'

Noah shook his head. 'I like everything you do. But I'd have taken it slower that first time. Been gentler.'

Her smile faded. 'Because I was inexperienced?' She inhaled slowly and he had the impression she was gathering herself. 'Did it make much of a difference? To your pleasure, I mean.'

His pulse tripped as he read doubt in her eyes.

Noah shook his head, sliding his hand into her hair and allowing himself one taste of her warm lips, slow and easy and inevitably arousing. It was an effort to pull back, especially when she kissed him back so sweetly.

'You have to be kidding.' She really *was* an innocent. 'I wasn't worried about my pleasure, but yours. For me it was fantastic. Exciting. Exquisite.'

She was exquisite. The tight, slick heat of her body, that impossibly snug embrace and the wonder in her eyes...

He shuddered, erection stirring.

That had to be why it felt so special. Because Ilsa had been a virgin, allowing Noah to be her first lover. That was sure to fire any man's libido. When coupled with her gorgeous body and her hoarse, sensual cries of delight, was it any wonder the experience felt extraordinary?

'I'm glad. I thought so too.' She lifted her hand to his collarbone, tracing a languid line down his pectoral muscle.

Pleasure jolted through him and he struggled for a

distraction, something to stop him using Ilsa's body again so soon when she might need time to recuperate.

'It was an honour, being your first.' It sounded old-fashioned and he'd never thought about that sort of thing. But knowing he was the first man Ilsa had given herself to, the first she'd wanted and trusted with her body... It made him feel remarkable.

'You're wondering why I took so long to have sex.'

He tried to read her expression but couldn't. For the first time since Ilsa had walked into his world Noah felt uncomfortable and unhappy at the sudden distance between them.

It was crazy. He didn't need to know her every thought. Yet with him she wasn't the polite Princess who masked her thoughts. He'd grown accustomed to a bright, sexy woman who was both fun-loving and serious, who didn't feel the need to hide herself.

'I'm curious, but it's no one's business but yours.'

Noah planted his palm across her wandering fingers and held them flat against his pounding chest.

Was she so unaware that she didn't know what she did to him with those beguiling caresses? Being naked in bed with Ilsa was testing enough.

'I like that you're not nosy,' she said suddenly. 'Lots of people think my life and thoughts should be an open book because of who my father is. As if I don't have a right to privacy.'

Noah had grown tired of media speculation about him since he'd become rich and successful. What would it be like, facing the limelight from birth?

'I'm sorry to hear that,' he murmured.

'It's not your fault.' Her eyes held his and he wondered if he saw wistfulness there. 'Staying a virgin wasn't deliberate. It just happened that way.'

Despite his determination not to be curious he couldn't prevent a stare of surprise. 'There must have been plenty of men pursuing you.'

She was warm-hearted as well as attractive, plus her social standing would draw many.

'Fewer than you'd think, especially since I live in the media spotlight. As you know, it's tricky, keeping a relationship private. Plus a lot of people are daunted by the idea of royalty, or can't see past the title.'

It was something she'd said before. That she wasn't just her title.

'How could anyone miss the vivacious woman behind the royal name?'

The flash of warmth in Ilsa's eyes spoke of delight and gratitude. Of a woman unused to personal compliments. How could that be?

'Some men aren't interested in the woman if they think the title can get them what they want.'

No mistaking her bitterness. Noah's jaw clenched as he realised she spoke from personal experience.

'You look so fierce.'

He worked to wipe his face clear of anger. 'Sorry.'

Ilsa inched closer. 'Don't be. I like that you're angry for me.' She paused. 'Even when I can fight my own battles, it's good to feel someone's on my side.'

A giant fist crushed Noah's lungs as he imagined her, alone, pitted against men who wanted her for her status.

'For what it's worth, a man would have to be a moron to value your title instead of you.'

Her arrested look revealed volumes. He wanted to scoop her close and tell her no one would hurt her again. As if he had that power. As if she'd cede that right to him.

'You really are nice, Noah.'

His brows rose at *nice*, but he couldn't cavil when she regarded him so warmly.

'I *did* fall for someone when I was in my teens. He swept me off my feet, or tried to.' Her mouth twisted. 'I was smitten and believed he was the love of my life. My parents weren't convinced and organised a holiday-cum-diplomatic tour with my mother. We were in North America for a month.'

She paused, her lips thinning. 'When we got home he'd gone. He'd tried to pressure me into bed and into an engagement, but he didn't even wait a month. Maybe he knew my parents had his measure.'

'You must have been heartbroken.' Noah's hand curled into a fist. He'd met some miserable excuses for men, but to take advantage of a teenager's romantic dreams...

'I thought I was, but I think I was just caught up in the romance of it.' She shrugged. 'The experience changed me. I wasn't so ready to believe every compliment. I became adept at discovering the reasons behind a man's interest. You'd be surprised how often it wasn't about me but about trying to get status or wealth, or even a bet about getting the goody-two-shoes Princess into bed.' She nodded at his indrawn breath. 'I became less trusting and less interested.'

There was still the fact that Ilsa had been engaged, twice, but hadn't slept with either fiancé. Even in the rarefied world of royalty that seemed odd, but Noah refused to ask. If she wanted to talk about that she would.

'Yet you trusted me. You let me lead you out from under the noses of all those gossipy socialites, straight to my yacht.' He dragged in a breath that hurt because his lungs had cramped, as he thought of the trust she'd placed in him. 'Everyone understood what it meant when we left together.'

No wonder the media had been rife with stories about them.

The risk she'd taken with him made him feel uncharacteristically humble. After her two failed engagements, the press eagerly extrapolated on the next instalment of what it saw as the ongoing saga of her love life. He'd risked nothing while she—

'It was different with you.' Ilsa slid her hand over his chest, covering the place where his heart thudded. 'I can't explain, but I believed you, and I wanted you, so badly. I'd never felt like that.'

'I know what you mean.' With her, everything felt different and new.

Noah gathered her in, not allowing himself to dwell on the idea that their relationship was unique, even though it felt like it. That had to be an illusion, maybe due to their phenomenal sexual compatibility. Yet he forgot about maintaining distance and revelled in holding her, naked and soft in his arms.

'You can trust me, Ilsa. I won't let you down.'

* * *

Ilsa knew better than to expect too much from a relationship founded on sexual attraction, yet Noah's words penetrated deep.

She heard the words and clutched them close, like a miser hoarding treasure. Would it really hurt to pretend, just for a short time, that what they had was real and more than a convenient affair?

No, it was too perilous. Just because she felt so much didn't mean this could last. Noah might be different from other men, he might make her feel special, but their paths lay in different directions. They lived on opposite sides of the world. He didn't want a family and she desperately did, though her chances of having a child were increasingly slim.

An ache started in her chest and she fought to suppress it. All she could do was live in the present. This glorious, amazing present. Later she'd worry about her future.

She snuggled nearer, inhaling the warm, spicy scent that was Noah's alone, determined to make the most of these incredible moments.

He rolled onto his back, pulling her so she lay over him, her head near his collarbone, her leg draped over his hip. It was remarkably comfortable. More than comfortable, she decided as she rubbed her face against him, fascinated by the texture of silky skin and crisp chest hair over hot muscle. He felt wonderful.

Yet Ilsa's thoughts kept straying to the fact that their lives would only intersect for a short time. This time together was precious.

'What are you thinking, Ilsa? It can't be good.'

She lifted her head to meet his questioning gaze. 'What makes you say that?'

'You're not relaxed any more.'

He noticed too much.

But Ilsa liked that. She'd never known a man so focused on her that he noticed minute changes in her mood. She propped herself up and stroked her palm across the plane of his jaw, adoring the hint of raspiness there.

She shook her head. 'Nothing really. Just about the fact this is an escape from reality. When this is over I'll have to go back to Altbourg.'

And try to carve out a new life for herself.

Noah's arms tightened around her. 'But not too soon.'

Those mesmerising eyes held hers as if willing her to agree. As if Ilsa needed persuading!

'No, not too soon.' She wanted to stay with Noah as long as possible.

'Do you enjoy being royal?'

Ilsa blinked. 'Enjoy it?'

'You look surprised. Hasn't anyone ever asked?'

'Never.'

'And?'

'It's the life I was born into. It's all I know.'

'I understand that.' He brushed her hair off her face as if to see her better then stroked his finger along her forehead, making her aware of her frown. 'But is it what you want to do? Does it make you happy and fulfilled?'

Noah Carson wasn't just sexy and compelling. He

was downright dangerous. With a couple of words he'd struck to the heart of Ilsa's problem. Though until now she hadn't allowed herself to think of it as a problem so much as passing restlessness.

'Sorry. I'm prying and I promised myself—'

'It's okay. Really.'

Except it wasn't. Not any more. Ilsa had spent so long telling herself everything would work out for the best because she was doing her duty, yet those words sounded increasingly hollow.

She lowered her head to his chest, listening to the thrum of his heartbeat beneath her ear. It was steady and reassuring, like the man himself. The man, she realised, she trusted. There'd been no vetting done by the palace, no discreet enquiries by her family, just her own instinct, yet Ilsa *knew* she could trust Noah as she did few others.

'No, it's not fulfilling,' she admitted finally. 'Not any more.'

Except for some of her projects, initiatives she'd got involved in by choice rather than because it was expected. Maybe that was where her future lay, pursuing those goals.

'But it was once?'

Noah wrapped his arms loosely around her, cocooning her in luscious warmth that counteracted the nugget of ice deep inside.

'To an extent. When I was young I had real purpose. For the first nine years of my life I was the heir to the throne. For as long as I can remember I was trained to lead the country. My parents and tutors aimed to mould

me into a queen who could lead the country through thick and thin.'

'Even when you were a kid?'

Noah sounded shocked. Ilsa heard indignation in his voice and felt...cared for. She let herself wallow in it for a second or two.

'Of course. It's easier to learn responsibility and duty early. There were lots of other things to learn too.'

Everything from languages, history and politics to etiquette and understanding her country and its people.

'But when you were nine that changed because your brother was born?'

'You've done your homework.' Ilsa circled a finger across Noah's ribs. 'As a male, Christoph became the heir.'

'It seems damned sexist that he took precedence, especially after all that time being the heir.'

Ilsa had grown up knowing what would happen if there was a male heir, no matter how unfair. 'Sexist yes, but constitutional change is slow and will probably take a generation to push through parliament.'

She paused, innate caution urging her to stop there. But she wanted to share with Noah. Besides, what she was about to say wasn't really a state secret.

'But it wasn't that simple. My brother wasn't well as a baby and he had health troubles through childhood. For a long time there was doubt he'd be able to inherit.' More than once they'd feared he'd die.

'He's okay now?'

'Oh, yes.' Ilsa smiled. 'He's grown into a remarkably strong young man.' At eighteen Christoph was full of

energy, making up for all those years of ill health. 'But until a few years ago that wasn't the case.'

'All that time you were still being groomed to take over from your father?'

She lifted her head and saw the implications register in Noah's expression. She nodded.

'And now you're suddenly just the spare.'

'Spare and surplus to requirements.' She shook her head as the words emerged. 'That came out wrong. I love Christoph. I'm relieved things have worked out well for him. I have no qualms about not inheriting the throne.' She paused. 'But it's strange not to have a clear direction and purpose any more.'

'So where does that leave you?'

She shrugged. 'Supporting my father and doing good works.'

Ilsa liked helping her people. She got a buzz out of making a difference, especially with social initiatives that the government considered too hard or too risky to invest in. It was the other duties, standing in for her father or brother, that she found increasingly frustrating. Because she wasn't valued for what she could contribute but simply as a royal placeholder.

That had to change. When she returned—

'You'd have been Queen if you'd stayed in Vallort.'

Noah's words jolted her, a reminder of her scandalous broken engagement. But when she looked at Noah he seemed lost in thought.

'Yet you decided against that and gave up another significant role you'd been groomed for.' His bright eyes

snared hers. 'For someone trained from birth to lead you must feel like your world has been tipped upside down.'

Relief scudded through her. He *did* understand. It felt like he was the only one who did.

'I'll adapt.' She had no choice.

'I'm sure you will.'

His confidence warmed her.

Yet it was difficult when the life mapped out for her hadn't followed the expected route. She'd been brought up to follow expectations. First there was being removed as royal heir, though she still gave thanks for her brother's recovery. Then the arranged match with Justin, Prince of Vallort. They'd known each other for years, and when he died she'd grieved for him as a friend.

But before she'd had time to adjust to that, the powers that be had demanded the engagement proceed, this time with Justin's heir, Lucien.

Ilsa had thought she could do what was expected. She liked Lucien. But even she, raised to expect an arranged marriage, refused to marry a man clearly in love with someone else.

So here she was, with no true vocation. No sense of purpose.

Something stirred inside, a twisting ache she'd tried to conquer, but it never quite went away. Ilsa might have been raised to rule but the secret she'd never shared with anyone was that she'd only ever had one dream. To be a mother. *That* she felt passionate about.

Her aspiration to have children wasn't something she discussed, especially not with her father. But it was one

of the reasons she'd agreed to an arranged marriage, hoping to make a family of her own.

Now that dream was in doubt. She was in her late twenties, with endometriosis and a family history of fertility problems. Her cousin, the same age as Ilsa, with the same condition, had tried unsuccessfully for years to have a baby.

Ilsa's doctor had warned of fertility issues. Her chances of having children grew slimmer with time. So when Lucien's ex-lover had turned up, pregnant with a baby she wasn't sure she could raise, Ilsa had considered adopting the child with Lucien. Until it became clear the pair were head over heels in love.

What would it be like to be loved like that? As if nothing else in the world mattered. She couldn't imagine it.

Noah brushed her hair in a soothing sweep that ended on her bare back. Ilsa arched into his touch, preferring to focus on the skin to skin contact than thoughts of what she didn't have.

She was otherwise healthy. She had her family and friends, a comfortable home and worldly wealth that made it possible to help others. She had much to be grateful for. Maybe that, she decided, would be her future. Putting into practise the social support schemes she hadn't been able to convince the Altbourg authorities to fund.

Talking frankly with Noah helped her see more clearly. It put in perspective what she really wanted.

She lifted her gaze to his, stunned at how good it felt

to share with a man who didn't judge her but simply made her feel good.

It was weak and dangerous to wish that this idyll could last. Their lives lay in separate directions. Yet she couldn't help wishing...

Noah watched her raise her eyes to his. She looked troubled. Despite her pragmatic words he'd caught an undercurrent of sadness in her tone.

'What are you thinking, Ilsa?'

He'd read between the lines and guessed at how momentous and unsettling recent events had been for her. He wanted to ask if her family had helped her. Had she had support? Did she discuss this stuff with them? Or was she supposed to suck it up and carry on alone?

Yet, as he watched, her mouth curled up at the corners. 'I was thinking how much I like being with you.'

His hold of her sweet body tightened. 'Good. I feel the same. I vote we stay and explore Istanbul before seeing more of Turkey.'

They hadn't discussed a specific time limit and he wanted to hear Ilsa say she wasn't in a hurry to return to Altbourg.

The need was selfish, because his hunger for her wouldn't be sated quickly. There was another element too. He respected her and wanted to help her, cushion her against the blows fate had dealt.

Had he ever felt that way about a woman? Somehow this didn't feel like a normal short-term affair. Unease flickered but he ignored it.

'You have time to do that? You had to work earlier.'

Noah had taken the video call instead of delegating because he'd needed some space from Ilsa.

'That was a one-off. I'm taking a break, remember?' He kept in touch with key staff, but with each passing day he relished his unaccustomed freedom. And his time with Ilsa. Deliberately he slid his hands across her silky skin. 'And we've got a lot of exploring to do.' He dipped one hand to her buttocks, pulling her against his growing erection.

So much for giving her time to recuperate.

Her breath caught. 'I like the sound of that.'

A tide of heat engulfed Noah as Ilsa wriggled into a more comfortable position over him. More comfortable for her. For him, it was torture of the most exquisite kind and a reminder that, despite her inexperience, they were equals in passion.

Everything about this woman, the shape of her body, the scent of her skin, the caress of her hair, even the way her mind worked, attracted him.

Noah's hands tightened on her hips. 'How tired are you, Ilsa?'

Her smoky gaze caught his. 'Not at all.' For good measure she rubbed herself against him. Slowly. Against his engorged arousal.

Noah shuddered and clamped her to him, lifting his rump off the bed as he slid against the slick folds between her thighs. 'You're a quick learner.'

'Does that mean I get a gold star?' Her cheeky grin faded as he cupped her breast, rubbing his thumb hard over her nipple so she gasped, thrusting towards him.

'You get whatever you like, sweetheart.'

'I want more.' She didn't sound so cocky now. Her voice was gratifyingly breathless.

'And I'm just the man to give you what you want.' If she'd said she was sore or tired he'd have had an ice bath. 'Reach over and get a condom.'

Even that was deliciously arousing as she stretched across him then sat straddling his thighs, a frown of concentration on her face as she tore off the wrapper.

'Can I do it?'

Touch him there? Absolutely!

He nodded then gritted his teeth on a hiss of breath as she fumbled it on.

Noah arched his head back against the pillow and tried to calculate mathematical square roots in his head. He didn't get far. Ilsa turned a necessary task into seduction. By the time she'd finished sweat had popped out across his brow and upper lip and he was rigid with the effort of holding back.

Slim fingers encircled him and slid slowly up.

'Do you like it like that or—?'

'I like it. But not now.' He was too close. Opening his eyes, he caught delight on her face. Time to turn the tables.

Noah removed Ilsa's fingers from around him and caught her other hand in his, then moulded both to her breasts. Surprise flashed in those blue-grey eyes, then understanding as he dipped his hand between her legs, slipping straight to her clitoris. She jerked against his hand and her fingers pressed against her soft breasts, her head arching back.

She was indescribably alluring. So sexy he wasn't

sure he could last long enough to ensure her pleasure as he urged her further up his body.

'Lift up on your knees.' Finally she was there, poised above his erection. Ilsa didn't wait for more instructions. She lowered herself and Noah felt the glide of taut, wet flesh surround him.

It was too much. He surged higher, hands anchored to her hips, securing her against him.

She felt so good he never wanted to let her go.

'Touch me, Ilsa.' The sight of her cupping her breasts and moving against him, her eyes a silvery blaze, was incredibly arousing. But Noah needed more of their connection.

She leaned forward, hands to his shoulders, breasts against his chest, and planted her mouth on his. The angle of his penetration changed and they were now body to body. Noah clamped one hand to her buttocks, the other to the back of her head, as he took her body and her mouth with thrust after delicious thrust.

Ilsa's moans were music. The restless circling of her hips the most potent aphrodisiac.

After two stunning climaxes he should be sated and lazy. Instead Noah was as desperate as the first time.

She writhed against him, all slender, sinuous femininity. He felt her quiver, her muscles tugging him, then suddenly there it was, like a freight train slamming over the horizon and straight at him.

Noah nipped at her lip, thrusting high and hard till she shuddered and convulsed around him, the sweetest torture of all. He swallowed her hoarse cry that might have been his name. Then the world smashed apart in a

blast of white-hot light and pleasure as he pumped his seed deep and hard.

When his mind worked again, Noah realised sex with Ilsa was the best he'd had. And it got better each time.

Why her? How could *perfect* keep improving?

Ilsa posed so many questions. Each hour with her seemed to increase his curiosity.

Just as well he had weeks to discover some answers. He sensed it would be hard to walk away until he had unravelled all her mysteries.

CHAPTER EIGHT

'THANK YOU, NOAH.'

Ilsa wrapped her arms around him, smiling in a way that made the sun seem to shine brighter. He drew her close in the shade of the trees near the ancient amphitheatre.

'What for?'

'Everything! This has been the most amazing day. The most amazing trip.'

Her eyes blazed bright blue, which he knew was a sure sign of happiness. He found it almost as attractive as the misty silver shine when rapture took her.

A familiar ripple snaked through Noah's belly, heading for his groin. He only had to think about sex with Ilsa to want her again.

Their desire for each other showed no sign of fading as they spent more time together. In fact, it seemed to build as familiarity deepened their connection.

'Amazing because we've seen lots of ruins?'

Today was a case in point. They'd come ashore and headed high up to the ruined city of Priene, perched below soaring cliffs and surrounded by pines that

scented the air. The place was deserted and magical, and he was glad to be here with Ilsa.

'You really don't mind, do you?'

For a second Noah managed to keep a poker face, then he grinned. 'I've enjoyed it all. Who'd have guessed scrambling over blocks of stone would be such fun?'

Seeing the old cities through Ilsa's eyes was a treat as well as an education.

They'd explored the grassy hillock of Troy, dotted with blood-red poppies, and she'd told him stories of the Trojan War and the archaeological discoveries made there. Further south they'd visited Pergamum and Ephesus, where he'd walked streets and visited homes erected thousands of years before.

Inland at Pamukkale they'd swum among fallen marble columns and soaked in warm thermal waters.

In between they'd feasted on wonderful food, met interesting people and spent days doing nothing more onerous than swimming off the yacht and having sex. Lots of sex.

'It's the best holiday I've ever had,' she murmured.

'Me too.'

Not that he'd had many. He'd spent years working every waking hour and though he travelled the globe, it was for business. His sexual liaisons were pleasurable but very short-term. He didn't take vacations with lovers.

Ilsa sighed. 'I could do this for ever.'

She leaned against his chest and he was surprised at his response. As if he too wanted to hold this moment and never let it go.

Noah shook his head at the fancy and stroked her ponytail of silky hair. His desire for Ilsa was as fresh as when they'd met.

Two people from such different backgrounds shouldn't be a good match. Yet their interests and personalities dovetailed beautifully.

She enticed and enthralled him and in many ways they were attuned. He respected her strength and honesty, her positive attitude and the way she treated others. She was genuine in a way so many people he met weren't.

But it surely these feelings couldn't last. Did this time with Ilsa seem special because it was the first real break he'd had?

'It's okay, Noah. I know it's not possible.' She drew back, a rueful smile on her face. 'But some moments are wonderful, aren't they?'

'I suppose they are. It's good to have a break from business sometimes.'

It was what his family had been saying for ages but it was Ilsa who'd made him realise it. Ilsa who'd given him a new perspective on his work-life balance and on his goals. He'd begun to consider some changes for the future.

'Business!' She stiffened and frowned, then looked up at him. 'That reminds me. Have you had time to follow up that contact in Altbourg I gave you? About a business opportunity there?'

Noah shook his head. He'd had other things on his mind. Namely her. And the intriguing new thoughts he was grappling with about what he wanted in his future.

'My PA sent a reminder. My father's office keeps asking. He's very eager about it.' Ilsa shrugged. 'But if you're not interested—'

'It's okay. I'll follow it up today.'

Damn her father for interrupting this idyll. Ilsa was so much more relaxed now than she'd been when they met. Noah would make the call so they stopped hassling her.

At that moment her phone rang and she frowned. She'd told him she had a new phone and very few people had the number. Part of her plan to switch off during this trip.

'Sorry, I need to take this.' She turned away and headed down the rows of marble benches. 'Hello? Lucien?'

Noah's fingers curled tight as he recognised the name. King Lucien, the man Ilsa had been going to marry.

He heard warmth in Ilsa's tone, and concern. A sharp, ice-hot sensation jabbed his chest. He breathed deep but couldn't dislodge the feeling.

Noah turned away to give her privacy, but an exclamation stopped him. He swung around to where she stood at the front of the amphitheatre.

Her shoulders were hunched and he wanted to take her in his arms. She looked so alone.

Despite their intimacy, there was a lot Ilsa kept to herself, as he did. Yet increasingly Noah found himself wanting to know everything.

Thinking of her with her ex-fiancé sent pain radiat-

ing through Noah's clenched jaw and deeper, where a phantom dagger jabbed his gut.

She and Lucien mightn't have been lovers but when Lucien rang Ilsa *had* to answer. Did she love him, despite what she'd said earlier?

Finally she ended the call and took a deep breath, tipping her face towards the sun as if seeking strength from its rays.

Because she pined for Lucien? Did she regret leaving him?

Noah took the steps at speed, his shadow falling across her face and making her open her eyes. The warmth in her gaze eased a tightness in his chest.

His hands closed around her elbows. 'Are you okay?'

'Of course.'

'But there's a problem.'

Her eyebrows arched, whether because he'd guessed or at his implicit question, he didn't know. This time he wasn't going to give her space.

'Things are getting complicated in Vallort and Lucien rang to warn me.'

Noah said nothing, waiting for more details.

He sensed Ilsa hesitate. Despite her forthrightness about many things, there were aspects of her life she guarded closely.

A noise made them look up. A group of tourists chattered and exclaimed as they approached. Noah led Ilsa towards the sheltering trees. When they were out of sight they settled on some marble slabs dusted with pine needles.

'Hear that?' Ilsa asked, looping her hands around her

knees. Noah tilted his head, registering the rustle of a breeze through the trees and a warbling bird. 'The peace here is incredible. No crowds, no press, no one expecting anything. Like the freedom of a ski slope at dawn.'

'That's why you've enjoyed this trip so much.' Amazing that he hadn't realised before. 'Apart from us being together. It's not just the historical sites but the chance to escape and be almost anonymous.'

Despite his high profile, he could still often be anonymous. Royalty was different.

Ilsa nodded. 'Yes. Being able to breathe and just be me has been wonderful.' She reached out and touched his hand. 'And being with you. Thank you, Noah.'

He didn't pause to examine that warm feeling inside. 'Something's wrong. Do you regret leaving Lucien?'

Noah felt her jolt of surprise, saw her eyes widen. 'I like Lucien, but it wasn't a good match.'

'And your first engagement? Was that a better match?' Maybe she still carried a torch for the fiancé who'd died.

Ilsa's scrutiny turned sharp and assessing. 'You want to know the truth behind my betrothals? The private story everyone is slavering for?'

Her words jabbed like blades. Damn right he wanted to know. But only because he cared about her. The thought of her pining over a lost love made him queasy.

Noah flexed his fingers, releasing her hand. 'I want to know what's bothering you, that's all. If I were going to sell a story about you I already have plenty of material.'

Her shoulders dropped as she exhaled. 'I apologise.

Hiding personal matters has become a habit. I don't really believe you'd do that.'

He shrugged. 'I understand. It can be hard to trust.' He too had developed a tendency not to admit strangers too far into his life. This connection with Ilsa was unusual.

'I knew Justin most of my life. I liked and respected him and was sorry when he died. Because I grew up knowing the marriage was expected it didn't seem odd. Especially as I no longer trusted my judgement of men or romantic love.'

'That makes sense.'

His doomed love affair had changed his whole outlook on romance, women and the notion of settling down.

Ilsa darted a look his way. 'The engagement to Lucien was another arranged match, to strengthen ties as our countries enter a new phase of economic cooperation and partnership.'

Surely that didn't require marriage? But then Noah didn't understand the workings of royal kingdoms.

'I liked Lucien but that was all.'

Noah felt a surge of lightness in his chest and head. Relief? Surely not. Or maybe just relief for Ilsa's sake.

'So you're not in love with him.'

'Hardly.' Her gaze shifted to the magnificent view just visible through the trees.

'But you're still in contact.'

Why did he push?

'We unleashed a furore when we split. It was a serious diplomatic incident. There was talk of not proceeding with the shared economic zone. On top of that the

media was desperate for details, making up stories when
they couldn't get the truth.' Her mouth turned down.
'They hounded Aurélie, the woman Lucien loves. The
lies they printed about her, saying she deliberately split
us up…' Ilsa shook her head. 'The vitriol only eased a
little when…'

She turned, her blue-grey gaze snaring his.

'When what?'

'When I let you sweep me off my feet.'

The press had been in a frenzy.

It struck him that Ilsa's decision to leave that party in
Monaco and embark on an affair had been very convenient for Lucien. It took the heat off him and his woman
since the press had to drop the 'poor Ilsa' theme that
had been so popular.

Noah's stare sharpened on Ilsa's face, but as the
thought surfaced he knew it was unworthy. She would
never give herself to a stranger to make a point for the
press.

'So Lucien and Aurélie benefited when you agreed
to sail away with me. What's the problem now?'

Ilsa's expression was wary. Had she heard the hint
of annoyance in his tone? She mightn't love her ex but
that didn't mean Noah had to like him. Ilsa had suf-
fered through this.

'Aurélie's pregnant but there's a complication. She
might lose the baby.' Her white face pushed any thought
of petty jealousy from Noah's head. He moved closer,
wrapping his arm around her, and she leaned in, making the tightness behind his ribs ease. 'She's in hospital
so there's no keeping it quiet. Lucien rang to warn me
we'd all be front page news again.'

'I see.'

For Noah, press interest had revolved around his success, or silly pieces about the world's sexiest bachelors. Neither bothered him. Ilsa's experience was completely different.

'It's not the press interest distressing you.'

Ilsa had already thumbed her nose at the gossips by taking up with him.

'I'm worried about Aurélie and the baby. She and Lucien have been through so much and this child means the world to them.'

Her mouth crumpled. She was such a warm-hearted, generous woman. Clearly she loved children, to be so worried about this unborn child. He remembered the dozens of cute slippers she'd bought for children in hospital, and the way she stopped to chat with kids wherever they went.

Is that what Ilsa wanted? Children?

Noah stared down into her troubled features and found himself crossing a boundary he hadn't intended to. But the pain he saw there dragged the words out.

'When we met I asked what you wanted from life. You said you didn't know. But you knew exactly what was important to you. Your people, your country and family.'

Her eyes met his, wide and wary. 'So?'

'Maybe it's time to put your people and your country further down your priority list.' He paused, trying to get a handle on his tangled thoughts. 'You want children too, don't you?'

Was that pain he saw in her face? Surely not, for abruptly she nodded and said softly, 'Yes. I'd love that.'

Everything inside him stilled. He felt poised on a knife-edge, watching emotions chase each other across her face.

Noah experienced a surge of unfamiliar feelings that made him hesitate.

He felt more for Ilsa than for any other woman. Even for Poppy, whom he'd once wanted to marry. But he'd changed since those days of naïve romantic dreams.

Noah told himself it was good to be aware of Ilsa's desire for a family. It was a timely reminder that what they shared, though spectacular, wasn't permanent.

Strange, though. That sharp phantom pain in his belly was back.

He raised his palm to her face, feeling tenderness well, understanding what a tough time she'd had.

'I can imagine you as a mother, Ilsa. You'll be wonderful with a family.' He paused and made himself go on. 'I hope you meet the right man for that soon.'

I can imagine you as a mother... I hope you meet the right man soon.

Noah's words echoed as Ilsa paddled her kayak in the early morning stillness. She heard them as clearly as if he'd spoken them now instead of days ago.

His meaning had been clear. *He* wasn't the man for her, not long-term. His plans for the future didn't include her.

She swallowed hard and dug in her paddle, skimming the surface and powering along the bay. She should be tired from lack of sleep, after another night spent making love with Noah. Yet she was filled with rest-

less energy, her thoughts darting uneasily to subjects she'd tried to avoid. Noah. The future. What she really wanted from life.

Once that had been easy. To serve her country and to have the family she'd always craved.

Now there was no defined role for her in Altbourg. None that would satisfy long-term, at any rate. As for a family, at her last gynaecologist's appointment she'd been told to prepare for the possibility she might not be able to have children. It wasn't certain, but time was against her. She shouldn't leave it much longer to try.

Ilsa breathed deep, acknowledging the inevitable wrench of pain and pushing it aside. But then came thoughts of Noah. Her generous, tender, fun, fascinating lover.

She'd never known a man like him. Had never trusted one so much. Never felt so much. She wanted—

Laughter rang out across the water then a babble of excited voices, including a deep masculine rumble that she recognised instinctively. Noah.

Ilsa was torn between the desire to join him and the need to be alone with her thoughts. Except those thoughts would be about him and she worried about exactly how deep her feelings ran for the deceptively easygoing Australian.

What had begun as an act of rebellion and freedom, a choice to indulge in pleasure, had turned into something that worried her. They shared an amazing affair. Fantastic sex, so fantastic it had opened her eyes to her own sensual nature. Camaraderie. Friendship, or so it felt. Caring too.

The problem was what else she felt for Noah.

So, instead of paddling further on her own, she turned towards the shore and welcome distraction.

The white sand beach glowed in the early light. At this hour, before all the visitors arrived, it was magic. The turquoise water was so clear that when she reached the shallows it looked like she was floating on air, not water.

Shouts rose and she turned to see several bodies hurtling down the beach, fine sand spraying from their feet. Noah's powerful form was surrounded by a gaggle of children. A football shot ahead and a boy yelled in triumph, outstripping the others.

Ilsa watched her lover keep pace with the rest of the group, accelerating enough to make the leader look over his shoulder and put on a burst of speed before aiming the ball between two piles of towels that marked an impromptu goal.

Noah had held back enough to let the boy score a goal, but not too much to be obvious.

She imagined him with his nephew, lolling in the yacht's lounge, engrossed in the computer game Noah had bought for his visit.

Ilsa couldn't imagine her father doing either of those things. When she and Christoph were young there'd been no noisy games in the King's presence. He'd loved and cared for them but in a rather distant way. He was more likely to reinforce a lesson in politics or manners than dirty his clothes with boisterous play.

Her childhood hadn't been unhappy but it hadn't been carefree. What would it be like to bring up a child

with someone like Noah? To be part of a family that cared and shared and wasn't focused on royal duty?

Everything she'd discovered about Noah indicated he'd be a wonderful father and supportive partner, if he ever changed his mind about settling down.

For a split second she let herself imagine it then tore her thoughts away, conscious of the dull metallic taste of disappointment filling her mouth.

'There you are. Just in time. We need another player to even the numbers.'

Strong hands grabbed the prow of the kayak as she reached the shore, dragging it up the sand. Then Noah was there, holding out his hand. Ilsa rose and, before she could step out, he lifted her and swung her high.

Laughter glinted in those sea-bright eyes and an answering smile tugged her mouth. Being with him made her feel good. As for being hugged close to that superb body... Sparks ignited deep inside as she nestled in his arms.

Ilsa couldn't have a future with him, but she could enjoy every precious moment together. The ache around her heart intensified. Last night, when they'd collapsed, sated and gasping on the bed, bodies humming with sensual satisfaction, Ilsa had found herself blinking back tears.

She wanted things she couldn't allow herself to want.

Noah's head lowered and her breath caught, anticipating the touch of his lips. Except the clamour of nearby children interrupted. With a wry smile he put her down on the sand.

'Later,' he promised, his lips softly burring her ear-

lobe, making her shiver. Then he straightened. '*Do* you mind evening up the numbers? If you'd rather not—'

'It looks like fun.'

She needed something to distract her.

They were a mixed bunch of varying ages and abilities. One child was so small that he fought back tears after getting caught in a tumble of legs as the older children vied for the ball. Noah swung him up to sit on his shoulders, from where he crowed his delight.

Ilsa found herself on a team with a number of girls, quick and light on their feet. One passed the ball to her and Ilsa took off, passing it when a teenager tackled her, then sprinting ahead, the wind in her hair and her blood pumping. Her partner passed again and Ilsa took a shot.

'Goal!' Noah's deep voice called out.

Instantly she was surrounded by cheering kids, a couple of girls high-fiving her and others dancing in delight. It was her team's first goal.

After that came several more, with Ilsa passing the ball again and again to beaming youngsters who managed to score. It was so long since she'd played group sport. She loved it.

'You have hidden talents,' Noah said as they stood on the shore, waving while the children headed off.

'Kayaking, you mean?'

His lips twitched and Ilsa felt it like a thread pulling tight inside her. She was so attuned to Noah that it was hard to believe they'd known each other only a matter of weeks.

'I was thinking of your football skills. I thought princesses practised curtseys, not kicking goals.'

'We're more versatile than you think. I mastered curtseys by the age of four. And I loved team sports.'

'You don't play now?'

She shook her head. 'Not since my mid-teens. Getting muddy and windblown wasn't considered a good look for the heir to the throne.'

And just like that the outside world intruded again, despite her attempts to keep it at bay.

Last night she'd had a message from her mother, saying her father deemed it time she return. Press speculation about her and Noah was causing headaches.

Her mouth twisted. They hadn't wanted her in Altbourg when she'd been a dutiful princess, because she'd attracted negative press. But now she'd broken out of the mould and was no longer seen as the goody-two-shoes Princess, they wanted her where they could keep an eye on her and manage the fallout.

She didn't want to go back.

She wanted to stay with Noah.

Ilsa swallowed. The truth sideswiped her.

Because she'd fallen for him.

A silent gasp snatched at her breath.

Ilsa had believed herself cured of romantic fancies in her teens. After that she'd accepted she'd marry for duty and that was fine because she'd lost faith in love. She'd loved once and almost made a disastrous mistake.

How could she think of going there again?

But it hadn't been an active choice. It just happened.

She squeezed her eyes shut, trying to control her whirling thoughts.

'Ilsa, what's up? Are you okay?'

She snapped her eyes open, met his searing turquoise gaze. 'Of course. It's just been a long time since I played football.'

Ilsa looked away down the beach, searching for something, anything to divert his attention. 'You're brilliant with children,' she said, hiding a wince. It was like probing a sore spot.

'That's because I've got a big extended family with lots of cousins. There's always a tribe of kids at any family gathering. At beach barbecues or backyard cricket.'

Before she could stop herself her mind conjured a vision of her and Noah on a vast Australian beach with a gaggle of family around them. She drew a breath and forced the image away.

'That sounds terrific.'

'It is. I'm looking forward to seeing them when I get home.'

Ilsa nodded and turned abruptly towards the kayaks. It felt like each movement was jerky and uncoordinated because of the effort of holding in her emotions.

'I don't know about you but I'm craving coffee. I think I'll head back.'

'Me too. Race you to the yacht?'

She pasted on a tight smile and pushed her kayak into the warm shallows, avoiding his eyes. 'You're on.'

But physical exertion didn't dim her agitation.

What was she going to do?

Noah expected her to stay another week or two, but eventually he'd leave her without a backward glance.

Ilsa couldn't handle that. Already she was wretched,

anticipating their separation. Staying would only make things worse.

Already she could barely hide her feelings and she refused to reveal them, only to evoke Noah's pity. Every hour they were together intensified her feelings and made it harder to face life without him. Better to make a clean break now than wait for Noah to tire of her.

She had been rejected first by the man she'd fallen for, because he couldn't be bothered waiting for her. Put aside as the royal heir, despite a lifetime's dedication and hard work. Palmed off to not one but two men who'd agreed to marry her only for the sake of their country, not because they'd wanted *her*.

Ilsa might have instigated the break with Lucien but he'd jumped at the chance to be with the woman he actually loved, the woman who was already carrying his child. That had slashed at Ilsa's ego. She hadn't wanted the marriage either, yet once again she'd felt unwanted, rejected at the most elemental level.

Her sense of worth had taken a hit, as it had when her father decreed she was a liability to her country.

She'd had enough rejection to last a lifetime.

Ilsa wanted Noah more than she'd ever wanted anything. Walking away from him would be appallingly hard. But it had to be done. Better that she walk away now than wait for him to call an end to their affair.

She needed to be alone. To lick her wounds and try to work out what to do with her life.

CHAPTER NINE

NOAH GROANED AND arched his head back under the streaming water. With one hand in Ilsa's wet hair as she knelt before him and the other flat on the wall of the shower, his body trembling on the brink of climax, he was stunned he could still stand. The hungry caress of her mouth drove him to the edge of sanity.

A shudder racked him.

'No!'

Somehow he managed to disengage himself, though the sight of her at his feet, lips parted and eyes hooded with arousal as she looked up at him, nearly sent him over the edge.

But some instinct stopped him. The same instinct that had seen him follow her below decks and barge into the bathroom where she was already showering. That had made him strip off and join her despite her wary expression.

For a second something had passed between them, a jolt of emotion he couldn't identify. Then Ilsa had dropped to her knees and taken him in her mouth and he'd lost the ability to think.

Thinking was beyond him now. But every instinct

screamed the need to possess this woman. Claim her as his, so often and so completely that she'd never run from him again.

'No,' he said again, his voice a guttural growl. 'I want *you*, Ilsa.'

There. That flash of silver in her eyes was surely a reflection of his own feelings. Noah let the sight reassure him as he dragged in a breath of sex-scented air and drew her to her feet. She was all gorgeous streamlined dips and hollows and long, lithe limbs. Her blonde hair was dark as a mermaid's tresses, plastered to her shoulders and the upper slope of her breasts.

He planted unsteady hands on her narrow waist then slid them towards her hips, ready to lift her up. But she turned in his hold. For a second he thought she was leaving. Just as he had when he'd entered the shower and caught surprise in her eyes that for an instant had looked like panic.

Instead Ilsa put her hands flat against the tiled wall, shimmying her hips back towards him.

It wasn't what he wanted. He needed to share the ultimate moment with their eyes locked on each other. He wanted that silent but powerful communion with Ilsa.

But then she shuffled closer, her legs splaying on either side of his, and Noah couldn't resist. He bent his knees and positioned himself between her thighs, one hand stroking her cleft and discovering her ready. So ready she tilted eagerly into his touch, her breath audibly catching.

He needed to know she was with him all the way, because he sensed that in the last half hour something

had altered. Something bothered her and he intended to find out what it was.

With one smooth, strong thrust he drove home. Right to her core. Right to the place where it felt as if he and Ilsa were one.

Delight was a ripple of excited nerves, a bunching of muscles and a tightening of flesh as she pushed against him, his name a gasp on her lips.

Next time they'd be face to face and he'd watch the flare in her silvery blue gaze as they orgasmed together.

Noah held her hips and thrust again, learning anew the rhythm and angle that ignited her blood, feeling her vibrate with excitement. This was what he needed. Weeks with Ilsa hadn't dimmed his hunger for more. For everything she could give him.

He wanted—

It hit him like a blast of summer lightning. He had an instant to feel Ilsa's muscles clutch him, then the burst of ecstasy as the tight, hard weight in his groin exploded into pulse after pulse of powerful delight.

Noah gritted his teeth and held on tight as he lost himself in rapture. The sound of Ilsa gasping his name. The indescribable perfection of them coming together in bliss. Starbursts behind his eyes. Silk and flame, roaring heat and almost unbearably exquisite sensation. And tenderness—tenderness more powerful than anything he'd known.

Finally, sighing and trembling, he bowed forward, bending over her, his arm around her waist, resting his head against hers, absorbing her heaving breaths into his own straining body.

Noah laved her slick shoulder then grazed the curve of her neck with his teeth and had to scoop her against him when her knees gave way.

Gently he pulled back and reached for the soap. Ilsa was limp, her eyes closed and breathing unsteady as he carefully soaped their bodies, then held her as the shower washed them clean.

Even then she stood silent, her head bowed as if from exhaustion. It was only when he turned off the taps and bent to lift her into his arms that her eyes snapped open, pupils dilated as she met his gaze. She huffed a deep breath and shook her head.

'I can walk.' Yet instead of moving she leaned in and brushed her soft lips against his. 'Thank you, Noah.'

He lifted his hand to cup her cheek but she turned away, stumbling a little as she pushed open the shower door and reached for a towel.

Noah had planned to take Ilsa to bed, to drowse with her in his arms, but she was already tucking the towel around her body and reaching for the hairdryer.

Disappointment stirred but he couldn't be selfish. She'd be more comfortable with dry hair.

He dried off, planted a kiss on her shoulder and another on the sweet curve of her neck, felt her tremble and smiled. He loved her responsiveness.

'I'll see you soon,' he murmured.

Noah left the room and threw himself down on the bed.

He should be exhausted after that stunning orgasm. Yet his brain was racing. What was on Ilsa's mind? Something was bothering her this morning and he in-

tended to get to the bottom of it. Not out of prurient curiosity but so he could help.

Noah cared for her. More, he realised, than he cared for anyone outside his family. So much that in the last few days he'd found himself dissatisfied at the prospect of their relationship ending soon.

Short-term affairs had suited him for years, yet now he found himself wanting more. How that could be achieved when they lived on opposite sides of the world he didn't know.

Of one thing, though, he was sure. He wasn't ready to say goodbye to Ilsa. It was time to think hard about what he really wanted from life, and from his lover. Meanwhile he'd talk to her about extending their cruise.

Every instinct urged him to protect her, especially as it seemed to him that precious few people had ever stood squarely on her side. Her family used her as a dynastic bargaining chip and her ex-fiancés... He gritted his teeth at the thought of them.

Ilsa deserved better than to be used. He knew exactly how that felt. He despised people who saw others as convenient tools to be manipulated for their own ends.

Poppy had used him for sex and the thrill of stepping out of her pampered cocoon to be with a guy from what she saw as the wrong side of the tracks. More, she'd tried to use him financially, wanting his money to finance her new business idea, believing he'd be so besotted he'd back her ill-conceived scheme when others wouldn't. In fact it was possible she'd targeted him originally for his money and the sex had been a bonus.

He'd been so bowled over by her he hadn't seen her

for what she was until she spelled it out for him. That he wasn't good enough for her. That she'd happily take his money but not his name. By which time she'd also hooked her claws into his little sister, with devastating effect.

Finally the bathroom door opened and Ilsa stepped in. To Noah's surprise she was wrapped in a robe with her hair not only dry but twisted up into an elegant knot, as if she were dressing for a formal function.

Ilsa hadn't worn her hair like that since that very first lunch when she'd looked like some untouchable ice princess. And, if he wasn't mistaken, she'd put on make-up, something she rarely did on the yacht.

He sat up against the pillows, watching her eyes widen as she took in his nakedness before turning swiftly towards the walk-in wardrobe.

She was getting dressed?

Noah frowned. The way her gaze had slid away from his made a phantom chill tickle his neck.

One of the things they both enjoyed after sex was lying in each other's arms. It had been a first for him. Before Ilsa he hadn't been into cuddles. But now he savoured the feeling of closeness he experienced with her. She'd always enjoyed it too.

Until today. Something *had* changed. He'd sensed it before and now instinct warned him it was more serious than he'd thought.

He paused, considering, then rose and strolled to the door. By the time he got there Ilsa was tugging a dress over her head. Not the floaty thing she sometimes wore over a swimsuit. A tailored dress. It screamed *serious* and *city*, not *vacation* or *relaxation*, much less *sex*.

Something turned hard and heavy in his chest.

A premonition of trouble.

It seemed impossible when fifteen minutes ago he'd been deep inside her, feeling her come around him. When five minutes before that…

Noah's fingers curled tight as he grappled with shock.

Ilsa was going somewhere. Every hair on his body rose as foreboding iced his blood. The urge to rip down the zip on her dress and pull her into his arms was almost overwhelming.

He propped his shoulder against the doorjamb and crossed his arms, aiming to look relaxed despite the tension screaming through taut muscles. 'Talk to me, Ilsa.'

She spun around and Noah saw emotion flare in her eyes. The tip of her tongue swiped her lips and he almost groaned aloud. She seduced him as no woman ever had, even when she didn't plan to.

He wanted to taste her, tease her, pleasure her. She'd enjoy it too, he knew. The awareness between them, the insatiable desire, was as strong as ever.

Noah stepped forward and she retreated.

That stopped him, a horrible sick feeling of shock hitting his belly.

'Ilsa?' His voice was a harsh scrape of sound. 'Are you going to explain what's going on?'

She nodded, her hands fiddling with a belt that accentuated her narrow waist. She drew a breath, lowered her shoulders and lifted her chin. Now she looked calm.

'Yes, of course. I meant to tell you when we got back from kayaking, but we were…distracted.'

She smiled but it was a perfunctory movement of her lips, leaving her eyes blank. As if the earth-shattering

sex they'd shared had happened to someone else. As if her throat and cheeks weren't still flushed from her orgasm.

Shock stirred that she should dismiss what they'd shared so easily. For it felt and sounded as if she dismissed much more. The closeness and trust that had developed between them.

He *knew* this woman, more than perhaps she realised. He'd read her responses to him. Heard truths she'd shared with no one else, witnessed the bond strengthen between them, *felt* her tenderness.

Noah stood straighter and watched her gaze skate down his body then back, not quite to his eyes. Was that fear he read there? That was another unwelcome shock. What was happening?

'Ilsa…' He moved but she stopped him with one raised hand.

'I have to go. I'm sorry to give such short notice but it's necessary.'

Another of those smiles that didn't reach her eyes.

'Short notice?' His gaze raked her, the sophisticated dress over bare legs and a body that probably still pulsed with the aftershocks of her climax. 'Don't you mean no notice?'

Stunned, he registered how she still refused to meet his gaze. This wasn't the Ilsa he knew. She couldn't be leaving by choice. 'What's happened?'

'I apologise. It's inconsiderate of me to leave without warning. But it needn't interfere with your plans. Once I'm ashore I'll get a taxi and sort out transport from there.'

'Talk to me, sweetheart. I can help you fix whatever it is.'

It was ludicrous to speak of leaving. Neither of them were ready for that.

She blinked and for a moment he thought he saw tenderness in her eyes. He hauled in a relieved breath until she shook her head.

'There's nothing to fix, but thank you all the same.'

Noah frowned, sensing something wrong. Something she wasn't saying. 'Listen, Ilsa, it needn't be like this. If people are demanding things of you…' He repressed the desire to say her royal parents had pushed her around enough, that they'd forfeited the right to dictate her movements. 'I'll help. You know I'll stand by you.'

Strange how easily the promise emerged. Their holiday fling had already changed into something else. In a few short weeks Ilsa had become important to him. If she were hurting—

'No!' She shook her head. 'I'm not being forced.'

She looked down at her clasped hands then back to him. 'Thank you, though, for the offer. And thank you for the wonderful holiday. It's been fun.'

Ilsa's voice was firm, almost businesslike in its crispness, and Noah felt his skin tighten. Because of her abrupt change of tone. And because Poppy had said exactly that when she'd dumped him. That it had been *fun*, but he wasn't good enough for her.

Noah tried to shove emotion aside and read Ilsa's expression. She didn't look worried or upset. In fact she looked totally composed.

As if leaving him meant nothing to her.

As if what they'd shared, all the things that he'd come to value, meant nothing.

Something plunged hard and fast from his chest to his belly.

He had a horrible creeping feeling of déjà vu but told himself it was impossible. Ilsa wasn't Poppy.

Yet looking into Ilsa's eyes was like looking at a stranger. Gone was all that lovely heat, the understanding and mischief, the sensuality and excitement. Instead there was…nothing.

Noah's brain blanked as he fought to reject what he saw and heard. It wasn't just her decision to leave but the way she did it, with no warning or explanation.

They'd agreed to a time-limited affair, but he'd swear she was nowhere close to being bored. Just as he wasn't ready to give her up.

But maybe, despite what he'd observed in the last weeks, he'd misjudged her. Perhaps, after all, she longed for bright lights and A-list parties with aristocratic friends.

A murky thought invaded his brain. Had he been wrong about Ilsa? Had she, like the woman he'd once planned to marry, been turned on by the novelty of a self-made man, and had that novelty worn off?

Had their desperate loving just now been a final titillating adventure before she moved on?

Every instinct rejected the idea. He *knew* Ilsa. She wasn't like that. He was *sure* she wasn't.

Yet past hurts crowded in, clouding his emotions and making it hard to think clearly. For the first time

in weeks Ilsa was hard to read, as if she'd deliberately locked him out. Noah *felt* her rejection like a slap.

And hadn't Poppy fooled him completely? Could it be that his judgement, so competent in business, was fatally flawed when it came to women? That, once more, he'd let his emotions override caution?

'What about *us*?'

He'd asked Poppy the same thing. The day she'd laughed in his face and sashayed out of his life to take up with someone whose background was suitably gilt-edged. It left Noah wide open, but he *had* to know.

Ilsa's expression closed even further, like a door slamming shut. 'There *is* no us.'

Like the thrust of honed steel through gathering ice, Noah felt disappointment and hurt meld into a sharp blade, piercing his chest and ripping down through his gut. He didn't want to believe it but the corrosive words spilled out.

'Because you're a blue-blooded princess and I'm a working-class guy? Because of my family background?'

Even as he said it, he wasn't convinced. There *had* to be some other explanation.

'It's not like that,' she said quickly. 'It's time I went back where I belong. My father wants me home now.'

Noah frowned at the mention of her father. Something niggled at the back of his brain.

The business deal her royal father was so keen on. The one she'd raised with him, then reminded him about when he'd been slow to respond. The one he'd promised to look into because he wanted her father to stop pressuring her.

Noah had been as good as his word, following through, investigating the possibilities and finally, *just yesterday*, after his team had researched it, signing an agreement for a joint project in Altbourg.

His nape prickled and he tasted something rancid on his tongue. It was too much of a coincidence. The morning after they'd got his signature on the agreement, Ilsa decided to leave. Had she been recalled by her father, after a job well done?

'Or is it time to go because you got what you really wanted, my name on the joint venture with Altbourg?'

Every instinct shouted it couldn't be true. Surely, confronted with such an accusation, she'd finally tell him the real reason she was leaving.

But all he got was a glacial stare. 'You *really* believe that?'

He didn't know what to think. That was the problem. The woman he'd grown to care for wouldn't treat him this way, use him to get what she wanted then go.

Ilsa wasn't acting like the woman he knew.

Maybe he didn't know her so well after all.

'I believe there's more to you leaving than you're letting on. Tell me what it is and I'll believe you.'

'Noah,' she said finally, 'I'd hoped we'd part as friends.'

'Friends? Friends trust each other. They support and respect each other. But I *know* you're lying to me.'

He watched her flinch, but still she said nothing. His mouth curled in distaste. Her silence spoke volumes. It didn't seem possible, but he had to face the fact that Ilsa wasn't the woman he'd believed her.

Why else would she refuse to explain? He'd offered to help her and he had the determination and resources to do just that.

'What's happened that you're needed so urgently? Has your father found you another aristocrat to marry?' His voice was harsh with hurt and rising anger. 'Or has your fiancé changed his mind and that marriage is back on?'

Ilsa stiffened, a pulse throbbing at the base of her throat. But still she said nothing.

Until this moment Noah had told himself he was wrong.

But she refused to contradict him.

Could it really be that she planned to leave him to marry a man she didn't love, simply to carry on their oh-so-pure bloodlines?

Or maybe, despite what she'd said, she'd been in love with her ex-fiancé all this time. Was that why she'd fallen like a ripe peach into Noah's hand, on the rebound?

Still he waited for her to say she didn't want to go. He'd gather her close and decide how to help her. Then they could stay together—

'I'm sorry you're upset, Noah.' She did up her belt in a couple of deft movements. 'I'll be packed and gone in twenty minutes.'

Then she turned and reached for her suitcase.

CHAPTER TEN

THE TAXI TOOK Ilsa to the airport. On the way she used her phone to book a flight out of Turkey. The next available was to London and she took it.

She didn't care where she went. Noah's burning eyes and lashing accusations had stripped her bare.

Ilsa could imagine only too well his reaction if she'd told the truth—shock and dismay. For he'd made it abundantly clear he wasn't looking for permanency.

She was shocked herself. Logic told her it should be impossible to fall in love with a stranger after only a few weeks. Yet it had happened and now she was stuck in this terrible limbo, yearning for a man she couldn't have.

Ilsa had opened herself up to him in ways she never had with anyone. Now she paid the price.

She hadn't thought it possible to hurt more than when she'd said she had to leave. How little she'd known.

When he'd lashed out at her, accusing her first of being a stuck-up socialite who'd dumped him because he wasn't royal, and then of using him to secure a business deal… Ilsa had wanted more than anything to set

him straight. To explain that he was the best man she'd ever known.

But then would come the questions, the demands. Noah wasn't the sort to take no for an answer, so she'd let him believe that ugliness rather than allow him to glimpse the truth. Because if he realised how much she wanted him he'd be *kind* to her and then she feared she wouldn't have the strength to walk away, pretending to be heart-whole.

She blinked furiously, fighting the tears glazing her eyes. She couldn't let them fall here in the taxi.

Ilsa shivered, folding her arms around herself and staring blindly at the passing landscape.

When she'd got aboard the yacht mere hours ago she'd dashed into the bathroom, needing time alone to sort out what to do. She'd wanted to face Noah fully clothed, hoping that would provide the armour she needed and help her hide her feelings for him.

When the shower door had opened and he'd stood there, tall, naked and aroused, and so incredibly dear, she'd known she fought a losing battle. She could no more tell him to go than she could fly.

She'd wanted to give him everything. To *show* him how much he meant to her, even if she didn't dare tell him. How his care and tenderness, as much as his eroticism, had changed her, giving her the strength to stand up for herself.

Her mouth had wobbled at the realisation she'd have to use that strength to walk away from him.

So she'd given him pleasure, dropping to her knees

and taking him in her mouth till he trembled and his powerful body stiffened on the verge of climax.

Yet he'd insisted they go there together.

That demand had nearly undone her. Which was why she'd turned her back on him, knowing she couldn't look into his eyes as they made love and not reveal her feelings.

Ilsa's body throbbed with the memory of them together, his hands clamped on her, holding her against him as he pumped so hard she felt it in her very marrow. She'd revelled in every thrust, every hoarse breath.

'We're here.'

Ilsa blinked and looked out at the airport. Despair engulfed her. She wanted to say she'd changed her mind and needed to go back. Would the yacht still be there? Would Noah let her aboard?

But it was impossible. Other women might believe in fairy tales about finding Prince Charming, who'd turn their life around. A princess born and bred, Ilsa knew fairy tales weren't real. The only person who could turn her life around was herself. Starting now.

Even if walking into the airport would hurt in every bone and muscle she possessed.

She paid the driver, smiled at his thanks and got out. She couldn't look back. She could only go on, even if she had no idea where she'd go or what she'd do with a life that now seemed grey and empty.

'I wish you'd reconsider, Ilsa. Your father…'

Ilsa didn't want to hear what her father thought. Not yet. Maybe not ever.

Noah had believed she'd been an agent of her father, using sex to persuade him into a deal her father wanted. That she'd dumped him as soon as he'd signed on.

A shudder ran down her spine. She wasn't ready to deal with Altbourg or the King.

'I'll be in London at least another week,' she told her mother as she curled up on a seat looking over one of the city's most exclusive squares. The view of green lawns and trees surrounded by impeccable white mansions was soothing. Ilsa was lucky to have the use of the house while her friend was away, travelling. 'But you can assure him that there'll be no more scandal about me.'

The press had gone wild with speculation, starting with photos taken on private phones in Monaco. Ilsa wasn't sure what had caused more fuss. The fact she was with another man soon after her broken engagement. Or that she, the demure Princess, had been seen with bare thighs, her hair loose and wearing killer heels.

She'd read some of the reports and, despite the puerile speculation, it was rather nice to be described as sexy, vivacious and even, in one case, as every man's secret fantasy.

It was a little balm to her wounded soul.

She didn't feel sexy or desirable.

'It wasn't the photos of you partying that concerned him, darling.'

No, it had been the fact she'd spent weeks with a notoriously sexy billionaire aboard his private yacht. The press had been breathless with wild speculation. Had she gone with Noah in the hope of making Lucien

jealous? Would the Altbourg royal family accept an Australian suitor? Her heart had cramped at that one.

The one good piece of news she'd had in the last week was a call from Lucien to say Aurélie and the baby were safe.

'Ilsa, did you hear me?'

'Sorry. I was a bit distracted.' She shifted, feeling that ache low in her back she sometimes got. She'd been tired and listless since arriving in London. Usually she soldiered on, even in pain. It was a luxury to relax.

'By Katrin's news? I'm not surprised. It's shocked us all.'

'You can say that again.'

Ilsa had taken a call from her cousin Katrin that morning, listening, dumbfounded, to the news that she and her husband were divorcing. Ilsa still couldn't take it in. The pair had been so happy. But years of unsuccessful fertility treatment had taken a toll and they'd recently been advised that further treatment was likely to be unsuccessful. Soon after, Katrin's husband had announced he wanted a divorce. He wasn't interested in adoption. He wanted a wife who could bear his biological children.

Horrified, Ilsa had offered to fly home to support her cousin. But Katrin was leaving almost immediately for a research job in the States and they'd agreed to catch up later.

They were close friends as well as cousins. Similar in age, they had shared similar symptoms and been diagnosed with endometriosis at almost the same time.

Ilsa was heartbroken for Katrin. As well, she

couldn't help wondering about her own fertility. She'd been putting off her next specialist's appointment. Now she realised she didn't want to hear what the doctor might say.

'I always liked her husband,' Ilsa's mother said. 'I'd never have believed it of him. They were so in love.'

'Love doesn't guarantee happiness,' Ilsa murmured. *It hadn't for her.*

She tucked her knees up against her chest. Life was delivering one blow after another.

'True.' Her mother sighed. 'But nor does an arranged marriage.' She paused. 'For what it's worth I thought that engagement to Lucien wasn't a good idea. I let myself be persuaded. That's no excuse, but...'

'What happened wasn't your fault.' Funny, to be the one reassuring her mother.

'Nevertheless, it was one thing, you agreeing to marry Justin when you'd known each other for years. It was another to expect you to marry his heir, no matter how useful it was diplomatically. We should have given you both more time.'

Ilsa's eyebrows lifted in surprise. It was the first time her mother had voiced doubt about something the King had decided.

'We've asked a lot of you over the years, darling. So I understand you needing a break now. I just wish you'd come home.'

A wave of warmth engulfed Ilsa. Her mother was worried, not because of the press or the political fallout from her actions, but because she cared.

'I'll think about it. But you're right. I need a break.

That's easier here where my PA can't schedule every hour of the day for me.'

Her mother chuckled and Ilsa heard amusement as well as concern in her voice. 'Fair enough. I'll talk to your father, try to divert him. But promise me you'll take care of yourself.' She paused. 'I could always fly over and keep you company.'

Like when Ilsa was a teenager and her mother had travelled with her through North America. But this time Ilsa didn't need time or distance to discover she couldn't have the man she wanted. She knew it all too well.

Her mouth crumpled as emotion clogged her throat.

'Thanks,' she murmured. 'But I'm fine. I just need a little more time.'

As she ended the call Ilsa felt the ache inside fill her to the brim. The heartbreak she'd felt as a teenager seemed absurd and insignificant by comparison.

She wished she could spend another day alone but the longer she holed up, the harder it would be, facing the public. She'd forced herself out once or twice this last week, but it had taken such effort.

Besides, she had an appointment she couldn't miss. One thing this time alone had given her was a chance to ponder what she wanted to do with her life.

Be with Noah Carson.

Ilsa winced and ignored the needy voice in her head.

She wanted to love and be loved. She wanted a long-term relationship and she wanted children. Which she wouldn't get hiding away. And if, as she feared, she couldn't have a family of her own, she could do her bit to help children in need. That had crystallised in her

mind after talking with Noah. Something positive she could accomplish.

This afternoon's appointment would be a step in that direction.

She lowered her feet to the floor and stood up, stretching.

Her heart might be broken, and she was still tortured by thoughts of the man she loved, but she had to try to get on with her life.

Ilsa stepped out of the conference room in the grand Mayfair hotel. She was glad she'd attended the session. It had been as interesting as she'd hoped and she'd made useful contacts. She'd stayed back talking with a couple of the presenters, one from New York and the other from Australia. Their stories gave her hope that a similar initiative might be feasible in Altbourg.

She smiled and nodded goodbye to the other attendees still milling around the foyer, turning to leave, and blundered into someone.

'Ilsa.' A hand caught her elbow and she froze.

For a second she couldn't look up, just stood, absorbing the feel of that large hand on her arm and the rough velvet brush of his voice trawling through her .

She breathed out slowly, searching for calm as her pulse skittered and her mouth dried.

'Noah.'

Finally she lifted her chin, drawn by a magnetism she couldn't resist.

Those eyes. As gorgeous as ever. That face, all strong lines except for his sensual mouth and the hint of a cleft

in his chin that accentuated his masculinity and at the same time made it seem more approachable, less over-whelming.

Except she felt overwhelmed. Totally overwhelmed.

Did he feel the fine tremors running under her skin?

His mouth crimped a little at the corners. An attempt at a smile or a grimace? Surely the last thing he wanted was to run into her.

'This is a surprise,' she managed, suddenly aware of the people around them. She snapped her eyes away from his and noticed several suddenly averted faces, as if they'd been caught staring.

Even here, in this bastion of the well-to-do, there'd be curiosity about their reunion.

Was that what this was? Excitement eddied deep inside before she squashed it. Of course it wasn't a re-union. Noah despised her.

'I thought I might run into you here.' His words yanked Ilsa's attention back to his face. And to the fin-gers still wrapped around her arm.

Why didn't he let go?

She wanted to think it was because he didn't want to. Because he craved the connection as much as she did, but she couldn't let herself fantasise like that.

'Really? How did you—?' No, she wouldn't go there. 'You're looking well, Noah.' Ilsa forced a smile. It was true. He looked fit, well-rested and heart-whole.

She feared she didn't. Sleep had been difficult this week because she'd grown accustomed to snuggling up against Noah's naked body. On his yacht sheer ex-haustion from their lovemaking had ensured she'd slept

wonderfully, whereas now she spent every night going over what might have been and what could never be.

'So are you.' Yet as his piercing gaze searched her face tiny vertical lines appeared on his forehead as if something perplexed him.

'Well.' She stepped back and he released her arm. Strange how her skin tingled from his touch. 'It's been good to see you but—'

'I thought you were heading straight back to Alt-bourg. Wasn't your family expecting you?'

She shrugged, not wanting to admit she still had no definite plan. 'I'll go home soon. There are people I needed to see first in London.'

He nodded. 'Ah, yes. Lord Brokebank. You looked very cosy on your date.'

'Breakhurst.' Ilsa's mouth tightened. There was no mistaking the steely note in Noah's voice. 'You've become a fan of the gossip columns, then?'

She and Antony had been photographed leaving a restaurant. The fact that the pursuing paparazzi had lost them in a traffic snarl had led to speculation that they'd spent the night together.

'Hardly.' Noah looked grim.

Ilsa tilted her chin. She refused to tell him it hadn't been a date. Antony was a financial guru as well as an old friend. They'd met to discuss her plan to endow an enterprise that, given time, would become financially self-sustaining and provide programmes for social change.

'What are you doing in London, Noah?'

His stare seemed to grow darker, even more intense,

and her breath seized. He'd come here to see her and, despite everything, a tendril of excitement budded.

Hectic heat rose in her cheeks as she remembered him taking his pleasure, and ensuring she did too.

'I have some matters to deal with before I head back to Australia.' Was *she* one of those matters? No. Their relationship was over. 'We need to talk in private, Ilsa.'

He kept his voice low, but she heard the steely note of determination.

Ilsa raised her eyebrows. 'Really?'

Injured pride surfaced. It didn't matter that she'd lied by omission, letting Noah think she'd used and discarded him. His accusations had hurt and she still carried the unhealed scars. How could he have been so ready to think her shallow?

But, instead of being deterred, he leaned closer. 'It's important, Ilsa.'

This close to him, she inhaled the spicy scent of his flesh. No other man smelled as good as Noah Carson. Dully she wondered if any man ever would.

Ilsa's heart skittered into an uneven beat, pounding high in her throat. Because the way Noah looked at her, with that searing intensity, told her she was his sole focus.

She tried and failed to rein in excitement.

What did he want to tell her?

Why the heat in his gaze? Was she imagining it? Attributing desire where there was none? Maybe he was simply about to announce his withdrawal from the business scheme in Altbourg.

But then, why the need for privacy?

'I'm not sure that—'

Someone bumped into her. At the same time she felt liquid splash her jacket.

'Sorry!' said a man's voice.

She looked down to see a massive patch of crimson on the pale raw silk of her jacket, dribbling down onto her skirt. A stranger stood beside her looking sheepish, an empty wine glass in his hand. She recognised him from the conference. Behind him a crowed of attendees were chatting over drinks.

'Here, Ilsa.'

Noah grabbed a napkin from a passing waiter and passed it to her. Their fingers tangled and heat shimmied through her.

He'd barely touched her, yet she felt it like a caress. Was she really so needy?

Despite everything, the answer was *Yes*.

While Ilsa dabbed at the stains, Noah said something to the man whose wine had spilled. The stranger apologised again and turned away. Then Noah moved closer, tall and broad enough to block her from the rest of the room. Sheltering her from curious eyes?

The action didn't fit with the angry man she'd left in Turkey. But today Noah was less like that suspicious man and more like the one she'd fallen in love with.

The realisation made all those emotions she tried to suppress rise to the surface. 'It really is time I left.'

'Please, Ilsa.' His voice, deep and full of sensual allure, stopped her. 'There's something you really need to hear. And you can clean up at the same time.' He

paused. 'The paparazzi are outside, covering the hotel entrance. It looked like they were waiting for someone.'

Ilsa sighed. 'Just what I need.'

If they saw her covered with wine stains they'd spin stories about her drinking too much.

Ilsa had promised her mother there'd be no more scandal. She didn't intend to add to her family's concern. Besides, she was planning some important initiatives. It would be easier to get people to buy into them and achieve her goals if her reputation wasn't the stuff of lurid press reports.

Noah held out his arm. It was such a familiar gesture. Ilsa wanted to lean into him and pretend, just for a minute, that they were still together.

No matter how she tried to ignore it, the air between them was thick with awareness. Her pulse thrummed too fast and between her legs moisture bloomed as every feminine part of her body reacted.

Because this was Noah, the man to whom she'd lost part of herself.

Ilsa forced a tight smile. 'Okay. I'll clean this and we can talk.'

That sounded simultaneously exciting and terrifying.

CHAPTER ELEVEN

Noah led her across the foyer, holding her close at his side and masking the stains.

Her breath shuddered out then snatched in so hard it hurt her lungs. Having Noah so near, feeling the heat of his body, the press of those strong limbs against her... She felt as unsteady as if she'd spent the afternoon drinking Schnapps instead of listening to presentations.

A few minutes later they emerged from the lift on a luxurious upper floor. There were just two doors in a corridor decorated with Venetian mirrors, vases of fragrant lilies and antique celadon ceramics.

She'd been so befuddled she hadn't thought this through. Now she turned to him. 'You're staying here?'

What were the chances of such a coincidence? Could he have booked a room because he knew she'd be here?

'Yes, I am.'

He opened a door and gestured for her to enter.

Ilsa hesitated. She wanted, badly, to be alone with Noah. Yet she shouldn't.

She looked up at his still form in the doorway. His expression was in shadow but she read tension in his jaw and shoulders.

A frisson of mingled warning and excitement tingled along her backbone. She could no more resist stepping over his threshold than she could fly to the moon.

Ilsa put her bag on a table inside the door and heard the door click behind her. Before her was a vast sitting room as opulent as a palace. For some reason she hadn't imagined Noah staying somewhere like this. Not because he couldn't afford it, but because she'd imagined him somewhere less traditional.

She was conscious of him just behind her, as if he radiated an energy that she registered like a burst of tiny explosions all across her skin.

'If you'll show me the bathroom...' She didn't turn, too hyper-aware of him just there, and of her craving to touch him.

Noah moved past her, so close she felt the waft of displaced air. Her gaze skimmed from his neatly trimmed dark hair to his shoulders, wider than ever in a jacket of dark blue, down to the swing of his arms and the easy stride of those powerful legs.

He didn't say anything, didn't look at her, and she told herself that was good. They weren't lovers or even friends any more.

So what did he want to discuss?

Ilsa swallowed hard, trying not to dwell on her tangle of disturbing emotions, and followed.

He led her to a magnificent marble bathroom. She blinked, telling herself it was because of the bright light, not because of the feelings bubbling inside. All because Noah was here, so close she could touch him. Making her want things she had no right to want. That old fa-

miliar craving was back, her body awakening to his presence.

Resolutely she stepped past him, crossing the space till she reached twin marble basins set in a bench that ran along one wall.

'Thank you, Noah. I appreciate this.'

Instead of meeting his eyes in the mirror before her she slipped off her jacket, studying the stain in the hope of distracting herself from Noah, so close, so tempting. Finally she put the jacket aside and surveyed her skirt. It would be almost impossible to salvage.

Ilsa thought of her promise not to attract any more scandal and drew a slow breath.

Glancing up, her gaze locked on Noah's in the mirror. She'd known he was still there because behind every scattered thought was a deep humming awareness. He stood in the doorway, one shoulder against the door-jamb, jacket open and hands in his trouser pockets.

The bare skin of her arms prickled as she realised her silk camisole was the same green-blue as Noah's eyes.

Not merely similar but exactly the same.

She'd bought the camisole days after arriving in London, drawn by the colour.

Had she bought it because it reminded her of Noah?

With difficulty Ilsa conjured a smile from tense facial muscles. 'I won't be long.'

Instead of replying, Noah silently straightened and took his hands from his pockets as if preparing to go. Ilsa wanted to say she'd changed her mind. She wanted him to stay. She'd missed him, thought of him every day and dreamed of him each night.

'Ilsa! Don't look at me like that.'

His voice was gruff and low and it made every tiny hair on her body stand erect.

Ilsa's pulse thudded. She planted her hands on the marble counter as her legs trembled. In the mirror he looked tall and daunting, his expression compelling.

'Like what?'

Her own voice was unrecognisable. Husky and breathless. Full of a longing she couldn't hide.

Slowly he walked towards her, stopping so close behind her she felt his body and more too, a tickle of sensation from her shoulders, down her back, buttocks and legs, as if he exuded a force field of energy. Except that tickle of awareness curled further, around her breasts to her peaking nipples and across her hips then arrowing down inside her pelvis.

Her snatched breath was sharp in the thrumming silence. Despite the way they'd parted her senses sang, being close to him.

'Like you want me.' He paused and it almost killed her that he stood so near yet didn't touch her. '*Do* you want me, Ilsa?'

She opened her mouth to deny it but couldn't.

Because it was true. She longed for him, despite all the reasons she shouldn't.

Long fingers skimmed her arms from her bare shoulders to her fingertips. It was like fire igniting and racing along a line of spilled fuel. Where he touched sensation leapt and heat burst.

Ilsa closed her eyes as delight coursed through her. How she'd craved his touch!

When their eyes again locked in the mirror, fear scudded through her.

This was wrong. There was no way forward for them together. It was better if she kept her distance.

She spun around, intending to tell him to move away. Instead her breasts rose on a gasp as she met the full force of Noah's stare. It spoke of desire, hot and enticing, and Ilsa melted.

His fingertips brushed back up her arms, the touch sure yet tender.

The locked-tight cast of his features eased into something softer. Even so…

'Noah. We can't. It wouldn't be right.'

Because she'd left him, and she feared being with him again would undo her completely.

'You think this doesn't feel right?' His voice was all gravel and whisky and enticement.

That fingertip touch dragged across her lace and silk camisole. Ilsa's breath snatched in and her breast lifted to his hand. Her mouth turned arid with anticipation as he skimmed her fullness then circled her aching nipple.

'Noah!' His name ripped from her lips and she didn't have enough pride to worry what that revealed. She arched, pressing closer, but still he refused to cup her fully.

'Say it, Ilsa.' His other hand skated around her other breast and she fought to remember why this wasn't a good idea.

She shook her head and grabbed his hand, telling herself she'd pull it away from her and end this torture.

Instead Noah leaned in, his lips against her ear in

a delicious caress. 'You want me to touch you properly, Ilsa?'

His caress turned from feather-light to deliberate and strong. He pushed up, taking her weight in his palm, capturing her nipple through her clothes and pinching gently till a fuse lit between it and her womb and everything ignited in a flash of conflagration.

Ilsa shuddered, the feeling so good she wondered for a second if she'd actually orgasmed just from his words and his hand on her breast.

But the hungry throb deep in her pelvis disproved that.

Holding her gaze, he circled her other nipple with his index finger and sparks swirled through her bloodstream. Any second now she'd combust.

'You want me, don't you?'

'Yes,' she gasped, goaded into abandoning her good intentions. 'Yes, *please*, Noah.'

He grinned then, dropped his hands and stepped back.

For a horrible, heart-stopping moment Ilsa thought he was leaving. That this was some sort of taunt, getting his own back on her for leaving.

Then, to her utter relief, he bent and skimmed the hem of her skirt high. Before her brain kicked into gear deft fingers hooked around her pantyhose and underwear, dragging them down her hips and thighs.

Ilsa clutched the surface behind her as Noah crouched low, his hand circling first one ankle then the other as he pulled her shoes off and the fabric free.

Breathless, she straightened, feeling cool marble be-

neath her soles. She reached for her waistband, then stopped as Noah lifted her skirt again. He bunched it up over her thighs and further, finally pinning the fabric to the flat of her stomach with his palm.

Eyes the colour of a tropical sea captured hers. Heat engulfed her in a whoosh of flame.

'My turn.' His teeth gleamed white against his tan as he grinned up at her. Then he leaned in, his breath stirring a flurry of sensation at the juncture of her thighs.

Firmly he pushed her legs wide. Then came pressure, delicious pressure from his lips and tongue.

Ilsa's head lolled back, eyes shutting as he pleasured her with such delicacy, such intimate understanding, that she felt the quakes building deep inside.

'Noah, please. I want *you*.' Ilsa ached for him, as she'd ached all the long, lonely nights, the hollow sensation within unbearable.

She looked down to discover her fingers clenched in his hair and those eyes, those paradise eyes, staring up at her between thick black lashes.

Still holding her gaze, he moved his tongue, slowly, deliberately, stroking her very nerve centre, and suddenly Ilsa was flying, the world blurring around her. All but Noah's eyes, watching her, holding her, keeping her safe as everything turned liquid and melting and ecstasy dissolved her bones.

When she came back to herself Noah was standing, pressed against her, holding her upright against something hard. She inhaled the spice and man scent she'd missed since Turkey and her throat closed on a sudden rush of tears.

'Ilsa?' He cupped her throat, his eyes questioning as they held hers.

In that moment she felt absolutely wide open and vulnerable. Every defence she'd ever erected around herself had shattered. Pride, common sense, caution, all gone. There was just her and Noah and the undeniable truth between them.

'I need you, Noah. Now.'

He frowned and she wondered if she hadn't spoken English but her native tongue. Then his hands firmed at her waist and he lifted her up onto the cool counter.

She sighed as he shoved her knees wide and stepped between them.

Ilsa's heart catapulted around her ribcage.

It was bizarre that he was still fully dressed and she was almost so. The slick flesh between her legs, swollen from arousal, was so sensitive even the brush of air as Noah moved felt significant.

But he only moved to reach into a pocket and draw out a square packet.

'You put it on,' he growled, pressing it into her palm so he could deal with his belt and trousers.

Ilsa's fingers trembled as she tore the packet and took out the condom. She was so eager she was clumsy, desperate to have Noah inside her. It took a couple of goes to get it right and unroll the latex around him. Noah didn't help her, but she heard the hiss of his breath as she covered him and guessed he was as desperate as she.

'Noah, I...'

Her words died as he kissed her. Hard and deep, yet

at the same time impossibly tender. Everything she was rose to meet him. Her hopes, her fears, her yearning.

Her love.

Ilsa wrapped her arms around him and kissed him back as if this were the last time.

Because she knew now what deprivation felt like. The time since they'd parted had been an emotional wasteland.

Now she came alive again, joy melding with arousal.

He pulled her to the very edge of the counter and the action brought her into contact with his erection. Excitement rippled through her, then, before she had time to do more than register anticipation, Noah was there, joining with her, pushing slow and deep until he sank right to her centre.

The weight of him, the sensation of them melding into one, was indescribably wonderful.

Ilsa blinked back tears and she kissed him with a desperation that bordered on wildness. Noah had touched something innate within her. He'd touched her heart, maybe her soul.

Her teeth grazed his tongue and bottom lip and he growled, his hands tightening satisfyingly on her body.

Finally he moved, taking up that smooth, deep rhythm she remembered from before. But this time it was a little uneven, his breathing ragged and his mouth fiercely possessive as he bowed her back in his embrace as if he wanted to imprint himself on her very being.

Tension rose. Wonderful, exciting tension that made her body clasp his in ripples of delight.

At the last moment Noah lifted his head, eyes fixed

on hers as bliss stormed her body. Ilsa clutched him with legs and clawing hands and couldn't hold back.

'Noah!' Her cry went on and on and on as the world turned again into that special place that only they could find together.

She heard him shout as he pulsed within her.

Coming down from ecstasy took a lifetime and Ilsa didn't want it to end. Even in bliss she knew reality would be tough. So she hugged her lover close, knowing that for this moment everything was all right. Explanations and solutions could wait.

Finally Noah stepped back, gently disentangling her and moving her back on the counter so she could slump against the mirror. Ilsa knew she was smiling. There was a gentle throb through her body, and it felt as if she'd run a marathon on legs made of marshmallow, but for the first time in over a week happiness filled her.

'Ilsa.'

She blinked her eyes open to find Noah standing before her. Trousers on and belted. Jacket neat on his shoulders instead of halfway down his arms where she'd pushed it. Only his rumpled hair hinted at what they'd just done.

In contrast, her hair had come down from its knot and lay around her shoulders. Her skirt was rucked up around her hips and her knees were splayed wide.

She shuffled her legs closed, tugging at her skirt to cover herself. Suddenly, without him holding her, she felt sticky and self-conscious. She wanted to slip down off the counter but wasn't sure her legs would support her.

Yet the truth spilled out. 'That was amazing.'

More than amazing. It felt like he'd changed her world.

Which he had. She cared so much for this man that even now Ilsa couldn't regret what had just happened. Even knowing they had no future.

Today had confirmed how deeply in thrall she was to Noah Carson.

Maybe she'd been wrong. Maybe she *could* cope with an affair a bit longer and somehow bury her emotions, working out a way to continue on with her life when they split.

Perhaps it was better to be his lover for a short time than not have him at all.

'It *was* amazing. But we have things to discuss. Important things.'

Ilsa read the decisive lines etched beside his mouth, the frown on his forehead, and foreboding stirred.

CHAPTER TWELVE

NOAH PACED THE suite's sitting room, waiting for Ilsa to appear. Surely, after their explosive union, this would turn out well.

He couldn't repress a smile. Their need for each other was stronger than ever. That *had* to be a positive sign. Today she'd come to him as naturally as breathing. As if she too felt bereft when they were apart.

Noah refused to believe she'd been with another man, despite the press speculation about an aristocratic lover in London. The idea sent an army of ants crawling over him.

Ilsa had been a virgin in his arms. Heat curled in his belly and his groin stirred at the memory of taking her across that barrier into experience for the first time. She'd been exquisite and sensuous, and it had felt like the world's greatest honour to be her first.

She'd lived without a sexual partner until so recently. She wouldn't start bed-hopping now.

No matter what he'd said in Turkey, Noah couldn't think of a woman *less* likely to give herself easily. Heat scored his flesh as he thought of the accusations he'd made, including that she'd used sex to seal a business deal.

Noah forked his hand through his hair, guilt biting at his conscience. He spun on his heel and paced the room again, reliving what he'd said to Ilsa. The memory left him feeling diminished and ashamed.

Long dead echoes of the past had risen, melding with new hurt and he'd lashed out, accusing her of using him, much as his ex had done.

Because Ilsa had taken him by surprise and he'd felt vulnerable and hurt. It was the very intensity of his feelings that had undone him. Because he couldn't understand her urgency to leave. He'd been desperate for her to stay.

Because he wanted Ilsa in his life. Wanted her long-term.

That was the truth he'd been grappling with just before she'd announced she was going. The idea would once have seemed outlandish. Now it made total sense.

Noah was the only one of his family in three generations who hadn't met and married his partner by his early twenties. Because, after his early mistake, he'd believed his judgement was flawed.

The Carsons had a tradition of instant attraction and lifelong devotion. Noah had believed he'd avoided that family trait since with Poppy he'd let lust blind him.

But now he couldn't ignore the signs. That immediate slam of awareness, unlike anything he'd known. His total absorption in Ilsa. The fact he'd upended his plans just to be with her.

He'd been happy for years to indulge in short-term relationships. All fun and no expectations.

That wasn't how he felt now. It hadn't been for some time.

So much hung in the balance. He couldn't recall

being so nervous before any business negotiation, but this was more important than any commercial deal.

A sound made him look up and he slammed to a halt, heart hammering, every muscle tensed.

Ilsa crossed the sitting room and sank into an arm-chair. Avoiding the sofas in case he sat beside her? His jaw tightened in disappointment.

Her posture was perfect, her head high. But her skirt was crumpled and stained, she'd put up her hair again but feathery tendrils escaped as if her hands hadn't been as deft as usual, and her mouth was swollen from passion.

She was the most beautiful woman he knew.

Noah's breath snagged in his lungs.

He hadn't intended to have sex with her before they spoke, much less do it up against the bathroom vanity. But his need had been urgent and so, he'd been grate-ful to discover, had hers.

Yes, surely they could sort everything out.

'Ilsa, I need—'

'Noah, let me say something first.'

She looked so serious that, despite the urgency gnaw-ing at him, he nodded and sat back. His apology was overdue but it could wait a few minutes.

'I shouldn't have left you the way I did, with no warn-ing. It was rude and it wasn't surprising you jumped to conclusions. But—' she leaned forward, her expres-sion earnest '—I never used you for gain. I didn't know about progress on that business deal. I didn't know you'd come to an agreement and it had nothing to do with me leaving.'

She looked at her clasped hands. 'I went with you

for purely selfish reasons. They had nothing to do with Altbourg or my father or business.'

'I know.'

She looked up, startled. 'You do?'

Noah nodded, tasting self-reproach on his tongue.

'I was in such a lather about you going I couldn't think properly. All I knew was that it felt wrong, you leaving like that. I lashed out with wild accusations and insulted you.'

He paused. 'That's why I needed to see you, to apologise. To tell you I'm sorry.'

'I see. Thank you.'

Yet she didn't look happy. He didn't blame her. She'd torn their idyll apart with her departure but he'd sullied what they'd shared and soured what had been special.

He still didn't understand why she'd run away, but one thing at a time.

'I appreciate you telling me.' She shifted in her seat as if preparing to leave.

'That's not all. You deserve to know the rest.' He drew a slow breath. 'I made the mistake of letting my emotions cloud my judgement and letting past experience prejudice me too. I'm sorry. I'm not making excuses, but I want you to understand.'

After all, honesty was the basis of a solid relationship and that was what he wanted with Ilsa. He was in for the long haul. As soon as he'd convinced her to take a chance on him.

If he gave her honesty, hopefully she'd reciprocate and share what was behind her leaving. He suspected it was because of demands put on her by her family or

royal obligations. He hoped to support to her with those but he had a lot of catching up to do.

Ilsa tilted her head as if trying to read his thoughts. He recognised it as her thinking look and something in his chest tightened at that endearing, familiar expression.

'I told you some people look down on my family because of the work they do.'

'And I told you that doesn't matter to me.'

Noah inclined his head. 'I remember. But the day you walked out was a shock to a man like me, used to being in control.' In business and his personal life things ran the way he wanted. Maybe he was growing spoiled by having his own way so often? 'It also reminded me too much of something that happened in the past. A woman who left me high and dry.'

The astonishment on Ilsa's face would have stoked his ego in other circumstances. It looked as if she had trouble imagining a woman leaving him.

But the joke was on Noah, for twice now it had happened and both times it had shifted his world.

He cleared his throat. 'Her name was Poppy. She was bright, sexy and fun and I thought I loved her, though now I suspect I was in love with the idea of love. I thought I'd found my life partner.' He shrugged ruefully. 'My family has a tradition of falling in love early and for life.'

'I see.' Yet Ilsa frowned.

'I'm sure you don't, but you will.' Noah drew a slow breath. 'Poppy didn't love me. It turned out I was just a bit of fun. A change from her sophisticated friends and

privileged lifestyle. I had money and a growing business reputation, so it didn't hurt to be seen with me. But when I asked her to marry me she was scandalised. She'd never lower herself socially to marry someone with a family like mine, despite all the lovely money I could provide.'

'That's truly horrible. I don't understand how you hadn't realised what she was like.'

A terse laugh escaped. 'I was very young and good sex can blind a guy. Besides, she was clever. She didn't make her feelings obvious, especially as she wanted me to fund a start-up enterprise she planned. An online fashion atelier.'

'She wanted you to lend her money?'

'Oh, not a loan.' He grimaced. 'She was insulted when I talked about drawing up a legal agreement. She thought I'd give her anything she wanted. Maybe that's part of the reason she took such delight in rejecting me.'

She hadn't held anything back in her scathing description of Noah and his family and he'd seen red when she'd insulted the people he cared most about in the world.

Ilsa said something under her breath in a language he didn't know. Yet he understood the sentiment and warmed at her outrage on his behalf.

'I'm sorry she hurt you and even sorrier that I reminded you of her. I see how my actions might have felt like an echo of that.'

'Thank you. I should have been able to shrug the experience off, but she hurt my family too. My sister in particular.' He'd never forgive her for the damage she'd

done to Ally. 'It's no excuse, but that day in Turkey was too much like déjà vu.'

'I'm so sorry.' It wasn't a platitude. He heard Ilsa's sincerity.

'It's in the past, or it should be.' Thankfully Ally was well and happy now, doing a job she adored. 'In the clear light of day I see that, but when we separated I let myself get swamped by doubt. I couldn't think clearly, even when instinct said you were honest and generous.'

'Our pasts affect us all.'

Ilsa's words made him respect her even more, and feel worse about jumping to conclusions. Ilsa battled to overcome her own rejections.

'You didn't deserve to bear the brunt of my temper.' Noah spread his hands and paused, knowing he needed to share something he'd never spoken about. 'The fact is I blame myself for what happened to my sister. I was the one who brought Poppy into her life. That's part of why I suspected the worst about you, even as I told myself it couldn't be true. It was unfair on you.'

'Thank you, Noah, and thank you for explaining. It makes things…easier.'

Did Ilsa's mouth turn down or did he imagine it? Suddenly, despite the desperate way they'd fallen into each other just now, Noah felt the full weight of trepidation press down on him.

'That's not the only reason I'm here, Ilsa.'

He felt his hands clench on the arms of the chair and relaxed them, trying to ease a little of his tension.

'I've done a lot of thinking. In fact—' he paused '—I've had a revelation.'

Noah studied Ilsa closely. Her body language warned him to tread very carefully. He hated even this small distance between them as they sat facing each other, but better to wait to reveal his feelings for her. Instinct warned him she wasn't ready for an emotional declaration.

This was a woman who'd been brought up to expect an arranged marriage, not a love match. He didn't want to scare her off by asking too much too soon.

She took duty seriously and he guessed she'd left because of pressure from her family. Noah planned to visit Altbourg soon and do everything he could to impress the King and win over Ilsa's family.

If that didn't work, he'd just have to sweep her off her feet and seduce her into staying with him. Because not having her in his life wasn't an option.

'Go on.'

'The fact is I've changed. Short affairs were fine for a while but I'm older now. My experience with Poppy soured my view of relationships for years. But our time together made me begin to rethink. It's stupid to make life decisions based on disappointment.'

He paused, trying to calm his now rackety pulse. 'I've realised I want more in my life. Children of my own and a wife.'

Her eyes snapped wide and he read shock in those bright blue depths. Did she have to look quite so stunned?

'Do you mean—?'

'It's okay, Ilsa, I'm not proposing. Or trying to tie you down.'

of the bodyguard she'd spotted when she left the hotel today. Not one of her own, for she'd ordered them to remain in Altbourg, but one of her father's staff. An unwanted reminder that, though she wanted a taste of freedom, she couldn't outrun her real life, even if she pretended for a week or two.

'Come back to mine.'

Those amazing turquoise eyes held hers and Ilsa felt a moment's surprise at how inevitable, how right this felt.

'Yes. Please.'

my word. Nothing will happen that you don't want to happen.'

Her breath hitched at the thought of what she'd like to happen. It was unprecedented to hunger like this for any man.

Ilsa tried to tell herself she was simply feeling bruised and rejected and Noah's blatant interest was balm to her battered ego. But the real truth swamped that totally.

The truth was she'd never in her life been drawn to anyone like this. Every cell in her body screamed that it would be criminal, impossible even, to turn away.

She moistened her lips and saw his gaze flicker and sizzle. In answer her breasts swelled, her already peaked nipples aching.

'It's Ilsa. Don't call me Princess.'

His sculpted mouth tilted up at the corners and that hint of appreciation undid another knot in the fabric of her defensive caution.

How would his lips feel against hers? Hot and decadent or coolly delicious?

'Shall we go?' His arm slipped from around her back, making her sway as if suddenly unsteady on her feet.

Or as if she didn't know how to hold herself without him touching her.

But he still held her hand and somehow, though his was larger and rougher, their palms and entwined fingers felt like a perfect match.

'Where to?' Ilsa tried to imagine taking him back to her hotel room, walking past the studiously disinterested gazes of the staff. And past the shuttered stare

Yet.

He could be patient. If that was what it took. He didn't want to frighten her off.

'I'm just saying my priorities have changed. You know I wasn't ready to say goodbye when you left. The fact is—' He shrugged, trying to look insouciant instead of mouth-dryingly nervous. 'The fact is I'm ready to start thinking about longer term and I'd like you to think about it too. I'd like to keep seeing you, find out how our relationship develops.'

She didn't respond, leaving Noah at the mercy of doubt and fear.

Finally Ilsa moved, lifting her hand and planting her palm against her collarbone in a classic, nervous gesture.

Noah breathed deep. Was it from surprise and excitement?

Everything—his future happiness, their future together—was riding on her reaction. He leaned forward.

'I don't know what to say.'

Ilsa pressed her hand to her chest as if she could prevent her heart from leaping free. She trembled with shock and excitement.

How badly she wanted to throw herself into Noah's arms, burrow close and feel once again as if everything were right in the world.

But she held back, trying to make sense of his words.

'Aren't you going back to Australia soon? How would a relationship work with you on one side of the world and me on the other? I have commitments here.'

And she planned on more with these new initiatives in the pipeline.

He smiled and spread his hands and pleasure darted through her. He just had to smile at her…

'Where there's a will there's a way. We can work the details out as we go if it's what we both want. It's what *I* want, Ilsa. That's why I came, to find out if you felt the same.'

She sucked in a desperate breath, searching vainly for calm. But how could she be calm when Noah spoke about long term? A possible future together. And family.

It was what she wanted. A dream come true.

Her blood fizzed with excitement and her heart swelled. She wanted to fall into Noah's arms, pepper him with kisses and show him how delighted she was at the prospect of staying with him.

Strange that she saw no answering excitement in his features. Instead his face was guarded and disturbingly unreadable. Even those gorgeous turquoise eyes seemed flat.

Ilsa surveyed him sitting there, feet planted on the floor, hands on the arms of his chair, no sign of emotion.

He looked like a man negotiating a business deal, not a lover waiting, breathless, to hear the *yes* he longed for.

Her elation dimmed.

She sifted his words and her heart sank.

Noah hadn't mentioned his feelings for her, just the fact that he had changed his mind about having a family. Come to think of it, he wasn't even saying he expected to be with her permanently, just that they should see how things went.

Like a try before you buy scheme.

Ilsa swallowed, horrified to taste a knot of tears high in her throat.

What had she expected? A declaration of love?

No, don't think about the answer to that!

'You're not saying anything.'

'You've given me a lot to think about.'

Noah wanted marriage and children.

Children.

Ice ran along Ilsa's bones.

'You definitely want a family?'

'Absolutely.' He smiled and *now* she saw emotion flicker in his eyes. At the idea of children.

Something dropped, hard and fast, through her abdomen, making her feel suddenly nauseous. She wanted a baby and the thought of having Noah's child would be a dream come true. But was it possible?

Ilsa had missed a recent gynaecologist's appointment, partly because she feared the prognosis. Her cousin's situation weighed heavily on her mind, and the fear that she too might also be infertile.

Then how would Noah react? He said he wanted a family and she read that truth in his eager expression. He looked more excited about that than when he'd suggested they stay together.

Through their weeks together Ilsa had seen him with kids often and knew he loved being with them. She suspected he'd make a great dad. When she'd asked what he enjoyed most he'd said being with his nephew.

If Noah wanted a relationship would it survive the possibility that she couldn't have children?

There were no guarantees, but she feared she knew the answer. Ilsa didn't think she had the strength to embark on a future with Noah and risk him rejecting her later for something over which she had no control.

If he told her he loved her then she'd scrape together the courage to tell him of her fears.

If he told her he loved her she'd brave anything.

But this wasn't a declaration of love. It was an invitation to continue their affair.

How would her heart fare if she stayed with him, loving him while he didn't love her? Knowing she might not be able to give him what he wanted?

Her life was already in turmoil. She had felt directionless, her confidence damaged and her sense of self-worth impaired by a series of rejections that weren't about her personally. How much worse would it be if Noah pushed her away?

Ilsa shot to her feet so fast she swayed.

'Ilsa?' Noah was on his feet too, just an arm's length away, his brow furrowed with concern. 'What is it?'

Her heart dived as she took him in. Tall and handsome but far more than that. He was the man who had unlocked her heart. And unwittingly broken it.

He reached for her.

'No! Please, don't touch me.'

Because if he did her willpower would crumple.

He reared back, palm raised, and she read shock flash across his features. It almost looked like hurt but that was her imagination. *She* was the one hurting.

'I'm sorry, Noah, but I can't. It's impossible.'

'Because of your commitments in Altbourg? We can work through that.'

Ilsa shook her head. 'It's not just that. It's everything. The truth is I can't see it working between us. We have different lives and different expectations.'

She wanted love, for a start.

After all she'd been through, all the disappointments, surely she deserved that. To be wanted for herself, just a woman, not a princess or a potential mother.

Even if she could have Noah's children, there was no reason to think she'd ever have his love. And she wanted that, so badly it terrified her.

Pain bloomed low in her body and spread slowly but inexorably until there seemed to be nothing left.

Noah moved closer, invading her space so she had to tilt her chin to meet his eyes. His warm male scent tantalised her, the fact that she could reach out and touch him and he would let her. But it wasn't enough.

'Think about it, Ilsa.' His voice dropped to that low note that always undid her. She had to stiffen her knees. 'We're good together. We can be even better.' He paused, his gaze pinioning her. 'You know we can barely keep our hands off each other.'

'This isn't about sex.'

'I agree. But you can't ignore what we already have.' Then he reached for her.

Stepping back was the hardest thing Ilsa had ever done. Harder than ending her engagement and facing pressure from the press, disappointing her family and her nation.

'Please, Noah. I said no and I meant it!' Her voice

rose, strident with distress, making him freeze. 'I don't want you to touch me again.'

Then, with tears blurring her eyes, she spun away, grabbed her bag and stumbled out.

It was only as she reached the ground floor that she realised she'd left her jacket behind and that she probably looked thoroughly debauched, perfect fodder for the paparazzi.

That was the least of her worries.

CHAPTER THIRTEEN

'IF YOU'D LIKE to sit here a little longer—'

'No, thank you,' Ilsa hurried to assure the doctor. 'I'm fine. I'm sure you have other patients.'

She'd probably already used up more than her allotted time. She got to her feet.

'Don't forget, tomorrow at nine. We can do the scan here. It's more convenient and private.'

In other words, the staff were discreet and there was less chance of rumours reaching the press.

Ilsa nodded. 'Tomorrow at nine. Thank you again.'

She emerged into a quiet boulevard with leafy shade trees. She drew a deep breath and walked briskly to her car. Ilsa preferred not to be photographed outside her doctor's office but she hadn't wanted an appointment at the palace, where it was impossible to keep a secret.

Instinctively she headed out of the city, driving on autopilot to a small country road and her favourite thinking spot looking across meadows and woodland to a shimmering lake.

A little while later Ilsa sat in the flower-starred grass and tried to absorb the peace that surrounded her. The

bright sunlight warming her. The song of a bird nearby. The sight of a couple of butterflies looping and wheeling across the wildflowers.

Yet her blood effervesced and her heart raced.

She was pregnant.

At first Ilsa had refused to believe it, because what were the chances?

It felt like a miracle.

It was, if not a miracle, an extraordinarily fortuitous event. That was the medical view.

If it hadn't been for that torn condom weeks ago in Turkey...

Ilsa sank back against the meadow grass and closed her eyes. Her breath hitched as tears spilled down her cheeks.

She'd never believed this day would come.

She hadn't dared to hope it would.

Even now she could hardly believe it, despite the doctor's assurance. The chances against it were so high.

Ilsa's hand crept across her flat abdomen and wonder filled her. Her tiny baby rested there. Hers and Noah's.

Behind closed lids she saw turquoise eyes, warm with laughter.

Noah, so caring and considerate, yet with a devil-may-care streak that she found impossibly enticing. They were qualities that would make him a wonderful father. He wouldn't be a stick-in-the-mud, too busy with work to find time for his child.

Noah would be a hands-on father. Ilsa could see him now, cradling a tiny baby against his strong body. Or teaching a toddler how to kick a ball.

Her heart dipped and she shivered despite the balmy sunshine.

But would he want anything to do with her now? She'd left him in Turkey and again in London, rebuffing his offer of a relationship. Ilsa shivered, remembering the pain and anger in his voice as he'd spoken of the woman he'd once loved. Who had spurned him and hurt his family.

Was that how he viewed Ilsa now? A woman who, despite her words, thought he wasn't good enough?

How she wished she'd been truthful and told him her real reason for rejecting him. Except it wouldn't have helped. He wanted a woman to give him children. He'd have politely but firmly rescinded his offer.

A cracked laugh escaped her dry throat. Ironic that she now carried his child.

Besides, that had only been half the problem. The other part was that she loved him and couldn't face a future pining for him to return those feelings.

How could they agree on sharing and supporting their child after what had passed between them? Especially when she wanted too much from him.

Ilsa tried to imagine telling him her news. Would he even see her after she'd walked out on him? Noah had been kind and warm-hearted before. But a self-made billionaire must have a formidable side. No doubt he could be ruthless as well as proud. Would he let her close enough to talk? Or would he reject her unheard?

She cringed, remembering that disastrous day in London. She'd escaped from the hotel's back entrance with the help of the manager who'd seen her emerge,

dazed, on the ground floor. He'd bundled her out of sight and ordered a trusted hotel driver to wait at the back entrance for her. They had been discreet, never breathing a word about her dishevelled and unconventional departure.

Since then she'd heard nothing from Noah. All she knew was that he'd returned to Australia and was making a splash escorting a parade of gorgeous women to one high profile event after another.

Yet she had to tell him about their baby.

Ilsa sighed. It would be the most wonderful thing in the world to share news of her pregnancy with the man she loved, if he loved her too.

But this was no time for fantasy. She grimaced. Noah probably never wanted to see her again. Plus— her heart pounded at the thought—she'd just been told her condition had to be closely monitored. Her chances of miscarriage were higher than average.

She lifted her chin and gazed at the pale blue sky.

All that was true. Things wouldn't be easy. But this was her miracle and she intended to embrace it.

'Noah?'

He stopped on his way into the conference room, turning to his PA. 'Yes, Bree?'

She got up from her desk, glancing at the open door. Only when she stood before him did she respond.

'I haven't had a chance to catch you in person. I wanted to double check. That instruction about personal calls still stands, doesn't it?' She leaned closer.

'No unsolicited private calls from women you haven't mentioned to me.'

'Oh, that. Yes, it still stands.'

Noah had learned to screen calls from women claiming to know him. Some were convinced that because he'd smiled at them in passing it was an invitation for an affair. The number who'd spun lies to his staff in the hope of getting access to him never failed to amaze.

His thoughts shot to Ilsa, the one woman he *wanted* to see. To the husky sound of her voice when she said his name. To the lilt of her laughter he'd missed so much. To her blank stare as she'd rejected him.

Pain clawed his belly.

But he'd resolve this soon, because seeing her again was a necessity.

He'd given her time but couldn't wait any longer. He'd engineered an invitation from her father. Did she know about that? It would give him the opportunity to see her in her own setting, get to the bottom of whatever stood between them, and prove to her that she needed him as much as he needed her.

He dragged his mind back to Bree. 'You know I don't have patience for time-wasters.'

'It's just…' Bree paused. 'I've taken some calls and I'm not sure if she counts as a stranger. Princess Ilsa of Altbourg.'

Ilsa? Calling his Sydney headquarters?

Shock slammed into him.

And something else. Excitement.

The woman bamboozled him. Undid him completely. She'd used and discarded him without a second glance.

Yet they'd had searing hot sex in a bathroom because she'd wanted him every bit as much as he wanted her. Neither had been able to wait to get horizontal on a bed.

The two actions didn't make sense together.

Nor could he easily lump her in the same category as Poppy. He'd *swear* she was different.

'When?' His voice scraped from a suddenly constricted throat. 'When did she call?'

'This morning. And yesterday.' Bree's wide eyes betrayed that she wasn't used to seeing her boss agitated.

Noah ran a hand through his hair, scraping his fingertips hard across his scalp, trying to get his blood pumping and his mind working. He felt dazed.

Why would Ilsa contact him now?

His heart gave a great leap and he scowled.

Instantly Bree shook her head. 'Okay, boss. I get the message. No calls from the Princess.'

Noah yanked a deep breath into his lungs. 'Did she say anything? What she wanted? Where she was?'

'Just that she wanted to arrange a meeting.'

Noah rocked back on his heels. A meeting? Not just a phone call? She didn't have his private number, as he didn't have hers. There'd been no need. They'd met and been inseparable.

His pulse quickened. If she wanted to meet, was she in Australia, or coming here? But what about those royal commitments that mattered so much?

Excitement scudded down his backbone.

'Don't worry, Noah. I'll fob her off if she calls again.'

'No!' Bree's eyes widened at his tone. 'If she calls put her through. And get her number.'

* * *

Ilsa watched the suburban houses blur through the bus window and tried to tell herself she wasn't being foolish hoping her news might change things between them. Would having a child together unlock tender feelings in Noah?

She bit her lip. Of course it was crazy. Even if Noah hadn't found another woman in the time they'd been apart, even if he was happy about the baby, didn't mean his feelings for her would alter.

Just as well an already broken heart couldn't break again.

She firmed her lips and shifted in her seat but that didn't stop her inner voice trumpeting unpalatable truths.

You still love him. And he has no reason to feel kindly towards you.

If she could turn back the clock…

No. She had to concentrate on the future. That was all that mattered.

She pushed down her sunglasses to look at the sign that gave details of the next stop.

Ilsa drew in a choppy breath. Not far now. She pushed her sunglasses into place and looped the strap of her bag over her shoulder.

Sunglasses, casual clothes and a ponytail weren't much of a disguise but so far they'd worked. She'd arrived in the country without fanfare, thanks to a friend who travelled to Sydney via private plane, and so far the paparazzi hadn't got wind that she was in Australia.

Her heartbeat pattered faster as she pressed the but-

ton for the stop, holding onto her seat as the bus swayed out of the traffic towards the side of the road.

Could she do this?

It wasn't ideal. Ideal would be her and Noah completely alone, but she'd take what she could get. Repeated rebuffs from his protective secretary meant Ilsa had no choice but to be creative in arranging a meeting.

Would Noah hear her out?

Had he given explicit instructions to bar her calls or hadn't he known she'd called? No point wondering now. She'd *make* him listen because he needed to hear this.

The bus stopped. Thanking the driver, Ilsa stepped out and put on a sunhat. Even with a cool breeze the Australian sunshine was bright.

Before her stretched a large park that fitted the picture Noah had painted when he'd spoken of weekend barbecues in the sun. There was an enormous children's playground plus shaded picnic tables and beyond those a vast parkland.

Fear clutched her heart and she breathed deep, willing herself into calm.

Surely, if the Carson family kept the tradition Noah had described, this was where they would be. The first Sunday of every month, regular as clockwork, he'd said. He'd even named the sprawling park where the clan gathered.

This was her chance to see Noah face to face. She couldn't imagine putting her news in an email.

Yet she couldn't imagine spilling it in front of his family either. Nerves tightened and her step faltered, but she kept going. What choice did she have?

Finally, she spied a group that might fit the bill. Tables were set up under shade trees but out in the sun were a number of tall, dark-haired men in amongst children and some older figures. One man in particular caught her eye. Even from a distance he was familiar. The set of his wide shoulders, the athleticism of that toned body as he loped forward and caught a ball tossed in his direction.

Noah!

Suddenly the absurdity of her plan struck her. Was she going to march up and haul him away from his curious family in the middle of a game?

Maybe she should wait till they took a break. Or was that cowardice?

Either way, she needed a moment to consider. She headed towards the trees when shouts made her turn.

A ball arced high through the air towards her. Instinct, prodded by a cry of, 'Catch it!', made her step to one side and cup her hands as it came straight towards her. Ilsa's hands closed around the ball and she heard applause.

A girl in her early teens ran up. 'Brilliant catch!' She grinned and held out her hand for the ball. 'Now it's my turn to bat.' She paused. 'Do you want to play?'

'I...' Ilsa looked past her to the heads turned her way. One in particular. Even from this distance she felt the heat from eyes that she knew were a stunning turquoise. It was an effort to drag her attention back to the girl.

'Please say yes. We girls are always outnumbered. I'm Jess and it's my birthday.'

'Hi Jess, and Happy Birthday, I'm Ilsa. I'm afraid I'm

not up to running at the moment.' She probably could but she'd take no chances with this baby. 'And I don't know the rules.'

'You've never played cricket?' Jess's eyes widened so much Ilsa had to suppress a laugh despite the tension winding through her body.

'I'm not from around here.'

'Now's your chance to learn.' Jess ushered her forward. 'It's simple. If you're in the field the aim is to catch the ball and get the batsman out. If you're batting, hit the ball between the fielders and run. But we'll get someone else to run for you.'

Ilsa let the words slide over her. Her attention was on the man who'd moved towards them then stopped, hands on hips as he watched them approach. Tall, imposing even in faded jeans and a polo shirt, the light breeze riffling his coal-black hair. Her heart squeezed. He was every bit as glorious as she remembered.

He surveyed her through dark glasses that gave nothing away.

'Ilsa.' His voice was deep and it ran like dark treacle across her skin, making her shiver.

'You know each other? Great!' Jess turned to the rest of the group. 'Everyone, this is Ilsa. She's joining us.'

Through the pounding in her ears Ilsa heard welcomes, but she couldn't acknowledge them. She was too busy staring at Noah, trying and failing to read his mood.

She didn't have to wait long.

'Ilsa won't be playing, Jess.'

He stalked closer. What was he going to do? Pick

her up and carry her away from his family in case she contaminated them? Her heart dived.

Noah stopped so close Ilsa felt the air sizzle with his tension. His jaw set hard and she *felt* his stare despite his reflective glasses.

'I'm not here to—'

Another voice interrupted. 'Welcome!'

Ilsa saw a middle-aged woman with greying dark hair and a familiar-looking face march towards them.

'Mum.' Noah didn't turn. His voice held a hint of exasperation. 'You don't understand. You don't know who this is. She's not here to play cricket.'

The woman stopped beside him, her gaze penetrating. Ilsa felt as if she saw straight through her efforts to look calm and right down into the morass of nerves and fear.

'Princess Ilsa.' Noah's mother smiled, reminding Ilsa heartbreakingly of Noah as he'd been all those months ago. Before everything went wrong. 'It's a pleasure to meet you. You're even lovelier in person than in the press.'

'Just Ilsa, please.' She felt flustered. Noah's animosity she'd expected. But kindness from his mother left her floundering. If Noah had told her about Ilsa, surely she wouldn't be so welcoming? Or had she only seen the speculation about them in the media?

'And I'm Joanne.' She shot a sideways look at her son and Ilsa saw Noah incline his head the tiniest fraction, as if giving permission. 'Would you like to join us? It's only a friendly game. We'll break soon to have lunch. Then the pair of you can catch up.'

Her simple generosity undid something deep inside Ilsa and her tangled emotions threatened to burst free.

She swallowed hard and didn't dare look at Noah, her feelings too raw. 'Thank you, Joanne. I'd like that very much. If you don't mind a raw beginner joining in.'

What followed was a revelation.

It shouldn't have been. The high-spirited game reminded her of playing football on the beach with Noah and the children they'd met. The game was hotly contested, with a high level of skill, but with camaraderie, jokes and kindness despite the occasional mock outrage and protests.

Ilsa's family loved her but they never shared anything like this. They didn't gather for barbecues or casual ball games at the weekend. The idea of her father taking time out to play sport with her or Christoph was unthinkable.

Yet that wasn't all that made this unique. Joanne had announced that Ilsa was a friend of Noah's, visiting from Europe, and that was all it took to be accepted. His family must be curious but instead of staring they drew her in, as if closing ranks around her. She felt accepted in a way that felt rare and precious.

Whatever happened after she and Noah spoke, Ilsa wouldn't have missed this for the world.

During lunch, Noah was busy at the barbecue, partly, Ilsa was sure, because Joanne kept finding work for him. It might have been entertaining, watching the decisive tycoon at the beck and call of his mother. Instead she found it sweet, because she knew he allowed it be-

cause he loved his mum. Seeing him with his family reassured her that he'd treat their child well, no matter how he felt about her.

She sat with Noah's cousin on one side and his sister Ally on the other. Ally was bright and engaging but clearly protective of her big brother, questioning Ilsa closely until Joanne intervened.

Ally apologised for being nosy, saying quietly that Noah had been her rock when she'd gone through tough times years before. Apparently he blamed himself, wrongly, for not protecting Ally better. She was convinced that he needed to concentrate on his own happiness now.

Ilsa ignored Ally's meaningful look but recalled Noah saying his ex had hurt his family and especially his sister. Seeing his close-knit family, she could understand why it was a sore point for Noah. Guilt swirled at how her rejection might have reinforced his negative feelings.

When Noah finally appeared beside her, Ilsa's pulse kicked up and nerves replaced the sense of wellbeing she'd clung to as a distraction from her inner turmoil.

Silently he reached out to help her up from the seat hemmed in against a table.

Ilsa stared at that strong hand, stunned at the friendly gesture, remembering how she'd spurned him in London. Colour flooded her cheeks and, before she could reach out, Noah dropped his hand to his side.

She scrambled to her feet, but he'd already stepped away and she felt a yawning hollow in her chest. It had just been a polite gesture for the benefit of his family.

Noah was already saying goodbye and there was a chorus of good wishes from his family.

'You have a lovely family,' she said when they were out of earshot.

'I know.'

His voice was tight and his face remained unreadable, but he didn't pause, though he shortened his stride to her pace. So she felt more comfortable? Or was it just a courtesy that had been drummed into him from an early age? Ilsa's mouth turned down. Probably the latter.

He gave no indication he was glad to see her.

She'd expected that, yet still she felt bruised.

'Where are we going?'

'Somewhere we can talk. Privately.'

He darted her a sideways look and something about it made her blood quicken. 'Where's your bodyguard?'

Of all the things he might have said, that was the least expected. 'At my hotel. I wanted…needed privacy for this.'

It hadn't been easy but she couldn't face doing this with a bodyguard in tow.

Noah nodded but he didn't look happy. Because he worried about her safety? More likely he was annoyed that she might have brought attention to his family. His next words seemed to confirm it.

'Hopefully you weren't followed.'

He surveyed the park as if looking for security threats or the photographers who followed her in Europe.

The lovely sense of freedom Ilsa had felt earlier dissipated. 'What about you? Don't you have security?' He was a wealthy, powerful man.

That provoked a laugh, warm and genuine, and the

sound swirled through her like a warm tide. 'You sat next to my cousin Jake at lunch. He's the head of my local security team.'

Ilsa could imagine it. Jake was big and solidly built but very fit and his gaze had been alert.

Her heart did a strange little tumble in her chest. Had Noah asked his cousin to look after her?

He led her to a car park and a gleaming blue vintage convertible. Ilsa stared, taking in its glorious lines. She knew there hadn't been many of these made and they had a reputation for great handling.

'Is there room for your legs?'

'More than you'd think.' He paused. 'What's wrong? You don't feel safe in a convertible?'

Ilsa met his narrowed eyes and shook her head. 'I was thinking how great it would be to drive the mountain roads at home in a car like this.'

Did she imagine a flare of approval in those sea-bright eyes? No. It was an illusion, gone already. Her mind was playing tricks and she couldn't afford that. Her positive experience with his family had skewed her thoughts.

Fifteen silent minutes later Noah ushered her into the lounge of a large house with a cliff-top view over the Pacific Ocean.

She didn't take the seat offered. She was too wired. Instead she moved to the large windows, trying to calm her breathing.

'So, Ilsa.' His voice, deep and powerful, scraped across her nerves. 'Are you going to explain what this is about?'

CHAPTER FOURTEEN

NOAH FROZE AS Ilsa stepped away from him. Her shoulders were high and she clutched that shoulder bag to her side like a protective shield.

She didn't want to be here.

He'd leapt to the conclusion that she'd come halfway around the world to see him. Now he realised, whatever this was, it wasn't the reunion he'd hoped for.

Bitterness filled his mouth. He should have learned his lesson by now. For all her fine words, Ilsa didn't fancy a future with a self-made Australian.

Yet still he'd hoped. He'd planned to see her in Europe. To persuade her, seduce her if need be, into seeing things his way.

It took everything he had not to reach for her. His palms actually tingled with the need to feel her satin skin.

She looked incredible, if a little pale, utterly gorgeous in casual clothes that took him straight back to the paradise days on his yacht when they'd been inseparable and the world had glowed around them.

But she didn't want him.

He remembered her dismay as he'd reached to help

her up from the picnic table. The hectic colour flooding her cheeks. How she'd looked away and kept her distance.

His stomach cramped. No wonder she'd been silent in the car coming here.

But after seeing her with his family it was clear that, she wasno snob. Poppy would have turned her nose up at mingling with them. Ilsa, on the other hand, had been a delight with them all.

This woman did his head in. She made him feel too much. For years Noah had called the shots, both in business and his personal life, but she left him reeling.

'Ilsa. Talk to me.'

Finally she swung around. Her closed expression and tight mouth made his heart hammer painfully.

She regarded him steadily, her gaze troubled. 'I'm sorry.' She swallowed. 'Walking out on you the way I did…' She shook her head. 'It was too much like the way Poppy behaved. I'm not surprised you don't want to see me.'

Ilsa remembered the name of his ex-girlfriend? Noah struggled not to feel it was important that she recalled such a detail.

He frowned. She was broadcasting conflicting messages. Obviously she didn't want to be here, yet she apologised as if sincere.

'You've got it wrong. I wasn't unhappy to see you.'

Ilsa shook her head, hurrying on. 'I'm sorry for intruding on private family time.' She lifted her chin as if in challenge. 'I tried organising an appointment but—'

'You don't need to explain. My PA has instructions

about fielding calls from people I don't know. I only found out you'd tried to reach me after she'd fobbed you off.'

'Oh.' Ilsa's tight shoulders eased down.

'I asked her to get your number if you called again.'

'Oh?' No mistaking her surprise. 'But you didn't want me there today.' Her voice was flat. 'You didn't want me to meet your family.'

She was right. Because he needed privacy to deal with Ilsa and resolve their issues. Trying to act nonchalant before his extended family, and his mother's appraising regard, had been almost impossible.

On the other hand, it had been an eye-opener seeing her interact with them. She'd seemed as relaxed and happy with some retired garbage collectors, a mechanic, a kindergarten teacher, a café owner and the rest as if she'd been at a party of sophisticates.

Just like when she'd played football on a beach in Turkey. Or chatted with fishermen or rug-sellers or anyone else she met.

Ilsa was what he'd thought her—genuine. The knowledge created a glowing kernel of warmth low in his body. A warmth he shouldn't feel, because what they'd shared was over.

'You took me by surprise. I thought you were in Europe.' Doing her royal duty.

'It's okay, Noah. You don't have to pretend. I realise—'

'I'm not.' He shook his head. 'It wasn't that I didn't want to see you, but a desire for privacy. If you came all this way to see me, it's not to play cricket with a mob of curious relatives.'

Ilsa's eyes widened and he saw a flash of silver there that catapulted him back to those times when Ilsa had looked at him with wonder and approval. As if his love-making had the power to change her world.

'You weren't trying to shoo me away,' she said softly.

Noah shook his head. 'I wanted to get you alone so we could talk.'

He paused, watching her absorb that and trying not to categorise his feelings. Because even now he felt far, far too much for this woman. Just seeing her, so close yet so untouchable, turned him inside out. He wasn't used to being at the mercy of emotions. He was used to being in control of every situation. Ever since Poppy.

'So, Ilsa. Why are you here?'

She might be good at looking calm and composed for the public, but Noah could read her better now. The hectic flutter of her pulse at her throat. The swift inhalation that lifted her breasts. The way she pushed her shoulders back as if preparing for something tough.

Noah felt himself stiffen in anticipation of bad news. Was she ill? But why travel to tell him when she'd washed her hands of him?

'Because I'm pregnant.' She paused and Noah heard the drum of his pulse in his ears once, twice, three times. 'We're going to be parents.'

'Parents?' His eyes locked on hers and it was like watching lightning flash down to earth. Ilsa *felt* the judder right to the soles of her feet. 'Us?'

'The baby is yours, Noah.' She grabbed for air then blurted out the truth. 'There's been no one else but you.'

He looked stunned. Who could blame him?

'That's why I'm here. I had to talk with you in person. I didn't want to tell you by phone or email.'

Not just because of her news.

Ilsa had *wanted* to see him. She craved the feel of his arms around her. His solid, reassuring presence. His smile that turned the world into an exciting, spectacular place. He'd accepted her as an equal, just as Ilsa, not because of her royal name or anything else. Had that man totally vanished or was some part of him left?

She waited for his response.

Would it be elation at impending fatherhood?

Wariness because he'd already moved on to a new relationship?

Or suspicion that she tried to pin a pregnancy on him?

She got none of those. Noah stood so still he didn't even seem to breathe. Yet that pulse of energy between them was like a live wire, crackling in the silence.

'Here.' Abruptly he took her arm and led her to a sofa near the window. 'Sit down and tell me everything.'

Ilsa was grateful for the seat. She'd screwed up her courage to come here and she'd ridden a wave of tension for too long. Her knees loosened and she plopped down onto the cushioned seat.

Noah took a chair opposite, leaning forward, his elbows on his knees. He looked intent, absorbed, but that was all. Ilsa had expected…fireworks. Delight or dismay.

Maybe because he didn't yet believe her?

'I suppose you'll want a paternity test.'

His brow furrowed. 'When did you find out? Is the baby okay? Are *you* all right?'

Ilsa put her hand up. 'The baby is fine so far and so am I. There's not even any morning sickness.'

She'd been tired, terribly tired, but she didn't know if that was from the pregnancy or the malaise she felt, nursing a broken heart and trying to find the enthusiasm to plan a future for herself and her baby. No matter how hard she tried, her mind skittered away from any concrete decisions. Maybe now she'd shared this with Noah she'd be able to focus.

He nodded. 'So, you conceived that day in London?'

'Actually, no. It was earlier.'

Ilsa looked down and realised she was threading her fingers together in a repetitive nervous gesture. The sort of gesture she'd been taught to avoid. But a lifetime's training in composure went out the window when she was around Noah. He tied her in knots so that everything inside seemed tangled.

'But the timing…' He shook his head. 'Just how pregnant are you?'

'Twelve weeks.'

'Twelve weeks?'

His gaze dropped and she realised her fingers were laced together, this time over her abdomen in an age-old gesture of protection.

'Why wait to tell me?'

Ilsa wished she could read his voice or his face. Work out what he was thinking. But there was nothing to hint at his emotions, apart from the intensity of his stare

and the way he canted towards her as if focused on her every word.

'In London it hadn't even occurred to me that I could be pregnant because we'd used condoms. My cycle is very irregular, so I didn't think it odd that I'd had no period. On top of that…' Ilsa looked past him to the vast ocean beyond the windows. 'I never expected it to be possible. I'd been warned I could find it difficult to have a baby. Plus you took precautions—'

'Except there was that one time when the condom tore.'

She nodded. She'd assumed at the time there was virtually no chance of her falling pregnant.

'That still doesn't explain why you waited to let me know.'

Ilsa couldn't read his tone, though that tall body looked primed and ready for action. But what action?

Nerves fluttered in her stomach. Noah was so *contained*, giving nothing at all away. A reminder that, while he might have been a phenomenal lover, a man who'd broken through her protective shell and made her dream of a fantasy happy ever after, he was a hard-nosed tycoon. He'd built his business from nothing and managed problems all the time.

Did he view their baby as a problem?

Ilsa sank further into the lounge, one hand resting on her abdomen.

She swallowed then moistened her lips with her tongue. Once more she sought comfort in the view of the ocean, rather than face Noah's piercing stare. Ilsa already felt too vulnerable around him.

'I didn't tell *anyone*. I thought it best to reach the twelve-week mark. The chance of miscarriage is greatest before that, so it seemed sensible to wait.'

There was movement in her peripheral vision then warm fingers covered hers.

Ilsa swung round to find Noah on the seat beside her, so close his masculine scent teased her and she felt she could dive into the clear depths of those stunning eyes. He was turned towards her, one long arm on the back of the lounge behind her head, his knee brushing her thigh.

'You were that worried you'd lose the baby?' His deep voice had a husky edge that undid her.

She nodded. 'I didn't dare hope. I've spent so long believing I'd have difficulty becoming a mother...' Her throat closed and just as well, before she blurted out more of what she felt.

'What do the doctors say? Is this dangerous for you? For the baby?'

For a second Ilsa couldn't speak, fighting the lush, warm feeling that filled her when Noah asked about her as well as the baby.

But it shouldn't surprise her. Noah was a decent man. Even if he didn't love her.

'I'm being closely monitored as I have an elevated risk of miscarriage.' She heard him suck in a sharp breath. 'But we're both doing okay and I trust my doctor to look after me.'

His tight grip fastened even harder around her fingers. Then abruptly he sat back, releasing her.

Ilsa felt it like the sudden chill when the sun disappeared behind a cloud on a winter's day.

'So everything's *not* good. But as good as we can hope for.'

Ilsa nodded, repressing a humourless laugh at the buzz of excitement she got, hearing him talk about *we* not *you*.

The trouble was that she still loved this man who, despite his concern, clearly wasn't excited by her arrival. She'd imagined he'd at least be thrilled to discover he was going to be a father. After all, kids were in his new long-term plan.

Had she allowed herself to hope that news of her pregnancy might magically erase the bad stuff between them? That he'd pull her close and whisper all those sweet promises she yearned to hear?

Who was she kidding? She'd dumped him when he'd offered her a future together. She'd kept her distance in case she lost the baby. Had she waited too long?

Ilsa shot to her feet and moved away. She put her palm on the wall of glass separating the luxurious room from the terrace with its infinity pool and sweeping lawn.

Dully she imagined Noah teaching a child to play cricket on that lawn or kick a football.

But she guessed it wouldn't be their child. Noah had shown concern for her health, and the baby's, but that was all. Duty rather than happiness.

Maybe he only had it in him to care for children by a woman he chose as his partner. Maybe he'd already found a new partner, one of those gorgeous women he'd been photographed with recently. Her heart dived.

'I came here to tell you about the baby and begin making arrangements so you can be part of its life.'

Ilsa turned to find him still on the sofa, his expression giving nothing away.

'But it's not as if we're a couple or live near each other.' She paused because she feared her voice revealed that she was crumbling inside. Then she forced herself to go on. 'So I understand if you've moved on and you prefer not to be actively involved.'

CHAPTER FIFTEEN

Not BE INVOLVED!

She had to be kidding. How could she even think it?

'You couldn't be more wrong, Ilsa.'

Her eyes snapped to his and emotion thumped his chest as he met that silvery gaze.

In the past he'd seen her eyes turn that colour when they made love, or when she was particularly moved. He'd believed it proof that she'd begun to return his feelings.

Now he wondered.

She'd avoided looking at him, preferring the view of the sea, but when she did he felt that familiar pulse of connection. The question was, did she?

Ilsa wasn't as calm as she pretended.

Deliberately Noah got to his feet, blocking the way to the door just in case. She looked so skittish.

'How could you believe that, even for a moment? Far from not wanting to be part of our child's life, I intend to be there every step of the way.'

Starting now. The thought of her miscarrying gutted him. Ilsa and their child needed him and he intended to care for them both through the pregnancy and beyond.

Her eyes grew round. What? She couldn't really have thought he'd walk away from her or his child.

His heart pounded like a jackhammer and his blood fizzed, and it was only partly to do with being near the woman with whom he'd planned to spend his life. The idea of becoming a father was the most exciting thing he'd heard in forever. He wanted to shout in elation. But not yet. First there was unfinished business.

'Why would you think I wouldn't care? That I'd ignore my own flesh and blood?'

She lifted one shoulder in a half shrug. 'Because it's *my* child and I spurned you.'

There was a shuttered look in her eyes that Noah hated. And something else. Pain.

It added to the ache deep inside him. An ache he'd carried since they'd separated. Telling himself she preferred to be with her titled friends and relations hadn't eased it and distance only made it worse.

'You think I hated you so much for leaving that I'd turn my back on my child?' Noah shook his head, holding her gaze. 'I admit it hurt.'

The moment she'd told him not to touch her had been one of the worst of his life. As if he'd been some bully using his superior size to intimidate her. As if she feared him. Everything inside him had shut down in disbelief.

Noah breathed deep, reaching for control, determined not to be railroaded by emotion. 'I knew you must have your reasons, even if I didn't know them.'

Ilsa frowned and Noah shoved his hands in his pockets. The time for prevarication was past. He was a proud man, but he'd learned love was more important than

pride. He wanted something better for them, and for their child.

'I checked into that London hotel because I discovered you were to attend a conference there on diversion programmes for young people in trouble with the law.'

Warm colour flooded Ilsa's face. Even her parted lips looked redder, and far too alluring. Noah wanted to grab her, tuck her close against him and not let her go.

But he leashed his inner caveman and focused on patience. Time apart from her had only reinforced his feelings. Life had been empty without Ilsa. He had to get this right.

'Now tell me straight, why did you leave? You never gave me a decent reason. Was it because of your family's expectations?'

Noah's eyes narrowed, his nape tightening and instinct prickling as she looked away.

When she turned back he stared into eyes of polished pewter, bright with troubled emotion. He sensed her turmoil, pain even, and wanted to reach for her, hold her close and support her.

But Noah stood still. He couldn't force this. She had to trust him.

'No, nothing like that.' Ilsa breathed deep and slow. 'I thought I couldn't be the woman you wanted.'

'Sorry?' He couldn't have heard right. 'I've never wanted a woman so much.' His mouth dragged wide in a reluctant smile so tight it hurt. 'With you I'm insatiable.'

He'd always had a healthy sex drive but with Ilsa...

'I don't mean for sex.' But he didn't miss the way her mouth curled at one corner, like a seductress proud of

her power. Even that made him hard. Everything about Ilsa aroused him. 'We both knew that it was a holiday fling. A short-term affair.'

'In the beginning, yes.' He frowned. 'But even in Monte Carlo there was no way on earth I could have walked away from that party without you. I've never felt anything like it with anyone but you. It felt like we were destined to be together. I spoke about a short affair because that's all I knew. But the fact is, right from the start, what we shared felt different.'

There, it was out in the open.

Ilsa's breath was an audible hiss. But he didn't read shock in her face.

Perhaps the notion wasn't new to her after all? Noah's pulse quickened.

'Was it like that for you too, Ilsa?' He'd believed so at the time but, if so, why walk out on him?

Slowly she nodded and Noah exhaled a breath he hadn't realised he'd held. His punished lungs eased and the constricting band around his chest vanished.

Noah stared at this complex, alluring, surprising woman and tried to get his brain back into gear. If she wasn't talking about sex, then...

'If you felt that way, why walk out on me in London? And don't say it was because of royal duty alone. I know that's important to you, but I know too that it doesn't completely satisfy you any more. I don't believe you'd turn your back on me only because your father crooked his finger.'

Ilsa squared her shoulders, her chin rising, and he *knew* she was fighting not to appear vulnerable. It made

his heart turn over. She might have secrets but in so many ways he knew this woman almost as well as he knew himself.

'When you spoke of long-term you said you wanted to try for a family and I knew how important children would be to you. I've seen you with kids time and again and you're a natural with them. I've heard you speak of your nephew and it's clear you love him. Your voice changes when you speak of him, did you know that?'

Slowly Noah nodded as, finally, some of the puzzle began to make sense.

'And you weren't sure you could have children.'

The realisation was simple but devastating. His gut twisted as he imagined how Ilsa had felt. He remembered how her face had glowed when she told him she wanted children. And today the stark fear mingled with determination on her features when she'd said there was a chance she mightn't be able to carry this baby.

Noah couldn't hold back any longer.

He took the step that brought them together, his arms wrapping around her, and it felt like coming home, even though she stood straight, not leaning against him. Her light citrus scent tickled his nostrils and he longed for the taste of her. Soon, he vowed. They'd clear everything up here and now. No more hiding or prevarication.

Ilsa was home to him in a way that no mere place could be. Being with her, he felt *right* for the first time in too long.

'You thought I'd reject you because you mightn't be able to have children.'

It was a statement, not a question, and the tremor he felt running through her confirmed it.

Ilsa had pushed him away, but how often had she been rejected? Once in her teens, then passed over for her brother, then recently spurned by a fiancé who'd chosen his lover over her. Of course she was wary.

'Oh, sweetheart, if I'd known.' He cupped her jaw, the better to meet her eyes. 'Yes, I want children. But I want you more.'

It felt good, finally to admit it.

Was that hope shining in her eyes? Or the over-bright glitter of unshed tears?

It made him wish he'd told her last time they were together. But then the realisation had been new to him and he'd still been grappling with the implications. Plus he'd convinced himself Ilsa wasn't ready for such a declaration.

'Noah.' Her voice was a husky whisper. 'I…' She shook her head. 'You don't have to choose now, do you? Now that I'm pregnant.'

The words pummelled him, opening up a yawning ache inside. How wary his lover was. How badly she'd been hurt to think that way. To imagine he'd choose a child over her.

Silently he cursed those in her past who'd made her doubt her intrinsic worth.

It felt like the most difficult thing he'd ever done, resisting the need to tug her closer. He settled for standing as he was, because nothing could make him pull back.

'I can understand you thinking that, Ilsa,' he said slowly. 'I can understand it might take months, even

years, for you to believe I care for you because you're the one woman in the world I want to be with for ever.'

Noah sucked in a breath and forced himself to face the unthinkable. 'Even if something happened to the child you're carrying—to *our* child—I'll still need you.'

Though he prayed with every fibre of his being that their baby would be safe and healthy.

'Even if you could never carry a baby, I'll need you. There's adoption. There are my siblings' and cousins' children we can spoil and help raise. There are plenty of kids whose lives we can help, even if they're not technically ours.'

He breathed deep, willing her to believe him. 'I can live without children, Ilsa. I can't live without you. These last weeks have been torment. That's why my mother welcomed you with open arms. She knows I'm a mess.'

Noah lifted both hands to Ilsa's still face, gently holding her jaw, brushing her cheeks with his thumbs and feeling the tremulous pulse at her jaw. Did she tilt closer into his hold?

'I love you, Ilsa. I've loved you from the first. Though it took a while to realise I'd joined the family club.'

'Family club?' she whispered.

He nodded, his soul shrinking as he read her doubt, her reluctance to believe him.

'The Carsons fall in love early. All the adults find their life partner by their early twenties. We have a tradition of long, happy marriages.'

'But not you.'

'Not until now. I'd been waiting to meet you.' That

was how it felt. 'With you it was like pieces of a puzzle finally falling into place. Even though I didn't want to believe it initially. It was easier to pretend it was just lust, easily satisfied by a short affair.'

Because he'd doubted his own judgement after his mistake with Poppy. Looking back, he suspected he'd fallen in love with Ilsa that very first evening, but the defence mechanisms he'd erected and his own stubbornness had stopped him realising till it was almost too late.

Reluctantly Noah pulled his hands away, knowing he had to give her space. 'But I understand I need to prove how I feel. You'll need time to trust me.'

A ripple of emotion crossed Ilsa's face and her mouth crumpled. 'I want to trust you, Noah.'

'I know, sweetheart. It's okay. I can be patient. I'll do whatever you need. You can stay in Sydney and see what life is like in Australia. There's plenty of space here.' He had a large home, too large for one person. 'Or if you'd rather not, I'll arrange somewhere else private for you. Or I'll come to Europe and find out about your life there.'

He paused, knowing he was in danger of rushing her. 'If you need more proof of my feelings, I'll get my assistant to send you my flight arrangements for the end of this week. I'd planned a visit to Altbourg. Ostensibly it's to scope that joint project. But in reality it was an excuse to see you.'

Her finger on his mouth stopped him. To Noah's horror he saw tears brighten her beautiful eyes.

'There's no need to persuade me.' Her soft words

were like a bar clanging down on his hopes. Wouldn't she even give him a chance to prove himself?

Then she smiled. It was strained and a little watery but so beautiful that his heart leapt.

'I want to trust you because I love you too, Noah. I've loved you since Istanbul. No, before then. I've been miserable, thinking of how I treated you and how you must despise me.'

'Oh, my darling.' Noah looped his arms around her and pulled her to him. Feeling her softness against him was like nothing else on earth.

But, before he could kiss her, she spoke again. 'You wanted to know why I left you. My possible infertility was just part of it.' She paused, her eyes dazzling as she met his look head-on. 'The main reason was because I realised in Turkey that I'd fallen for you, hook, line and sinker. I was scared, Noah. Scared that I wanted so much more than you did. I was afraid if I stayed with you—'

This time it was Noah who stopped her words with his hand. He felt her soft lips against his fingers and the sensation sent fire streaking through him.

'If only I'd known.' He shook his head. 'It was in Turkey I'd begun to realise I wouldn't be satisfied with an affair. I was already planning to ask you to stay longer when I found you packing, determined to leave straight away. That's why I was so savage. What I felt for you, what I still feel, is far beyond what I've ever experienced before.'

'Noah, my love. I've been such a coward. I should have told you. You mean so much to me.'

He'd never heard anything so beautiful in his life. Or seen anything more glorious than Ilsa, looking up at him, eyes blazing with love and joy.

Tenderly, careful of this precious woman, Noah gathered her to him and kissed her gently, allowing all his adoration to show.

'I want you more than I'd ever thought it possible to want, Ilsa. I'd give up everything else to be with you.'

Her hands anchored on his shoulders and he felt her rise on tiptoe, kissing him with a sweet insistence that healed the pain of separation.

Finally, when they pulled apart to gulp in oxygen, she spoke. 'You don't have to give up anything, Noah.'

'And nor do you. Whatever it takes to make this work, I'll do it. Maybe relocate to Europe or—'

Her lips on his tasted like paradise and he lost his train of thought. But that didn't matter because Ilsa was here in his arms, and she loved him.

'We've got all the time in the world to make those decisions, Noah.' She paused. 'But I've got one condition I do insist on.'

His head jerked back and he surveyed her through dazzled eyes. 'Name it.'

His groin tightened as she pouted and lifted her hand to the buttons of his shirt. 'I'd like a tour of your home. Specifically, the master bedroom. It's been ages...'

'But in your condition—'

'The doctor didn't put a ban on sex, you know. And I've missed you so very much.'

For answer Noah swept her up into his arms but his laughter faded as he looked down into her dear face.

'I love you, Ilsa. Whatever the future brings, I'll always love you. I'll strive to make you happy.'

'You already do, Noah. So much I feel like my heart might burst.'

'You took the words out of my mouth, sweetheart.' Then he strode to the door and the beginning of their life together.

EPILOGUE

'THE VENUE IS just as spectacular as I remember from last time.'

Ilsa's mother smiled as she stared through the soaring windows of the Sydney Opera House. Beyond, the harbour stretched like midnight silk towards the bridge, proudly illuminated against a dusk sky of neon pink edging to indigo.

Beside her Joanne Carson nodded and sipped her wine. 'The old Coat hanger still looks good, doesn't it? One of my uncles used to be a rigger up there, decades ago.'

'A rigger?'

The pair were soon engrossed in stories about work on the iconic bridge, and Ilsa felt that warm glow she'd experienced the day her mother and Noah's had met and immediately struck up a friendship.

Around them theatregoers were dressed in everything from evening finery to more casual yet dressy outfits. Some had recognised their group, craning to get a better view. A visit to Sydney by the King and Queen of Altbourg was seriously newsworthy. Plus the

press never seemed to tire of photos of Noah, Ilsa and their son.

But the intense, almost breathless reporting of their romance had eased since their wedding in Altbourg's main cathedral last year and then little Oliver's birth.

Ilsa glanced at the familiar suited security officer just beyond her mother and mother-in-law. And then across to Jake, Noah's cousin, on her other side. He nodded and grinned. He'd confessed that the first time he'd attended a ballet in his security role he'd expected to hate it. But now he had a newfound appreciation for the athleticism and artistry involved.

'What are you smiling about, sweetheart?'

Noah's warm voice rippled like molten caramel through her body. She turned and there he was, as breathtaking as ever.

Her husband. Her man. Her other half that made her whole.

Ilsa's heart leapt as she read the smile he reserved just for her.

'Thank you.' She accepted the glass of sparkling wine he held out. 'I was just thinking about how we've changed your cousin's life. He's now a fan of ballet as well as cricket and rugby.'

Because Noah always kept his wife and mother company at the ballet.

'It's good to expand our horizons, like me taking up snowboarding.'

Noah had taken to the slopes in Europe so easily it was hard to believe he hadn't been born to it.

'Or my father learning to change a nappy,' Ilsa added.

She couldn't stifle a giggle at the memory of King Peter's pride when he'd announced that he'd changed little Oliver.

Maybe it was the chance to relax away from the royal court, but she saw her father more and more as a man, and a doting grandfather, than a royal. Tonight he and Noah's father had been eager to pack the rest of them off to the ballet. No doubt they planned to settle in the media room, babysitting Oliver and watching football over a beer. The growing friendship between the two families was more than she'd dared hope for.

Ilsa and Noah spent part of the year in Australia and part in Altbourg and so far it worked well. Noah said the months based in Europe were a bonus to working in the region. Meanwhile, Ilsa pursued her passion for helping vulnerable children in both her home countries and further afield.

But her main passion was her own family.

How blessed she was.

Warmth slid around her waist as Noah pulled her close, his arm coming to rest on her hip. Instantly her pulse thrilled and her mouth dried.

'Have I told you how beautiful you look, my love?'

'You have.' Frequently. 'But don't ever stop.'

'No chance of that.'

His eyes danced as he surveyed her. From the lustrous, large Australian pearls at her ears and throat—a gift from Noah—to the new silk dress in the colour that had become her favourite. A unique blue-green turquoise that matched her beloved husband's eyes.

As she watched he frowned, his mouth tightening, and she felt a shudder rack his tall frame.

'What is it, Noah?' Alarmed, she put down her glass and pressed her hand to his chest. 'Are you unwell?'

His mouth hooked up at one corner in a rueful half smile. He bent so his words feathered her ear. 'Just impatient. I need you alone, naked, in bed, as soon as possible.'

He straightened as her pulse shimmied to a decadent tango beat as she imagined being naked with Noah. Ilsa's eyelids fluttered. 'We could leave. Our mothers would barely notice.'

'Is that the voice of my dutiful Princess?' There was laughter in Noah's voice but love in his eyes. 'Imagine the explanations. No,' he said decisively. 'We'll wait. There's only one act to go. And I'll make the wait worthwhile, Ilsa.'

'You promise?'

'Have I ever let you down?'

She shook her head. From the moment they'd acknowledged their feelings to each other, he'd been everything she could want in a companion, lover, partner.

'Never, darling.'

Ilsa smiled and, ignoring the curious glances, pressed her lips to his, clinging for a few luxurious seconds as he wrapped his arms around her.

The world was already full of photos of them kissing. What was one more?

* * * * *

Swept up in the heat of

Claiming His Virgin Princess?

*Don't forget to check out the first instalment in
the Royal Scandals duet*

Pregnant with His Majesty's Heir

Also don't miss these other Annie West stories!

The King's Bride by Arrangement
The Sheikh's Marriage Proclamation
A Consequence Made in Greece
The Innocent's Protector in Paradise

Available now!

COMING NEXT MONTH FROM

♦ **HARLEQUIN**
PRESENTS

#3985 BOUND BY HER RIVAL'S BABY
Ghana's Most Eligible Billionaires
by Maya Blake
Why, wonders Amelie, does she feel such a wild attraction to Atu? He wants to buy her family's beach resort, so he's completely off-limits. Yet surrendering to their heat was inevitable...and now she's pregnant with his heir!

#3986 THE ITALIAN'S RUNAWAY CINDERELLA
by Louise Fuller
Talitha's disappearance from his life has haunted billionaire Dante. Now he'll put their relationship on fresh footing—by hiring her to work for him. Yet with their chemistry as hot as ever, will he ever be able to let her go again?

#3987 FORBIDDEN TO THE POWERFUL GREEK
Cinderellas of Convenience
by Carol Marinelli
The secret to Galen's success is his laser-sharp focus. And young widow Roula is disruption personified! Most disruptive of all? The smoldering attraction he can't act on when he hires her as his temporary assistant!

#3988 CONSEQUENCES OF THEIR WEDDING CHARADE
by Cathy Williams
Jess doesn't know what she was thinking striking a just-for-show arrangement to accompany notorious playboy Curtis to an A-List wedding. What will the paparazzi uncover first—their charade...or that Jess is now expecting his baby?

HPCNMRA0122B

#3989 THE BILLIONAIRE'S LAST-MINUTE MARRIAGE
The Greeks' Race to the Altar
by Amanda Cinelli

With his first bride stolen at the altar, Greek CEO Xander needs a replacement, fast! Only his secretary Pandora—the woman he holds responsible for ruining his wedding day—will do... But her touch sparks unforeseen desire!

#3990 THE INNOCENT'S ONE-NIGHT PROPOSAL
by Jackie Ashenden

After everything cynical Castor has witnessed, there's almost nothing he's surprised by. But naive Glory's offer to sell him her virginity floors him! Of course, it's out of the question. Instead, he makes a counter-proposal: become his convenient bride!

#3991 THE COST OF THEIR ROYAL FLING
Princesses by Royal Decree
by Lucy Monroe

Prince Dimitri's mission to discover who's leaking palace secrets leads him to an incendiary fling with Jenna. As their connection deepens, could the truth cost him the only woman that sees beyond his royal title?

#3992 A DEAL FOR THE TYCOON'S DIAMONDS
The Infamous Cabrera Brothers
by Emmy Grayson

Anna has spent years healing from her former best friend Antonio's rejection. Then a dramatic fall into the billionaire's arms spark headlines. And his solution to refocus the unwanted attention? A ruse of a romance!
